T0209963

CHINA DOG

CHINA DOG
AND OTHER TALES
FROM
A CHINESE LAUNDRY

JUDY FONG BATES

COUNTERPOINT

First U.S. edition published in 2002 by Counterpoint
First published in Canada in 1997 by Sister Vision Press

Portions of this book have previously appeared in slightly different versions in the following magazines: "My Sister's Love," *Fireweed* and *This Magazine;* "The Good Luck Café," *Canadian Forum*.

Library of Congress Cataloging-in-Publication Data
Bates, Judy Fong, 1949–
    China dog and other tales from a Chinese laundry / by Judy Fong Bates.
      p. cm.
    Contents: My sister's love—The gold mountain coat—Eat bitter—Cold food—The lucky wedding—The Good Luck Café—The ghost wife—China dog.
    ISBN 1-58243-188-4
    1. Ontario—Social life and customs—Fiction. 2. Chinese—Ontario—Fiction.
I. Title.
PR9199.3.B375724 C45 2002
813'.54—dc21
                                      2002022791

Cover design by Amy Evans McClure

COUNTERPOINT
2560 Ninth Street Suite 318
Berkeley, CA 94710

ISBN: 978-1-58243-188-8

Printed in the United States of America

FOR MY PARENTS

CONTENTS

1

MY SISTER'S LOVE

MY SISTER'S ARRIVAL IN CANADA HAD THE EFFECT of a cleaver, slicing up our lives. Three years earlier, my father had sponsored my mother and me to Canada. My mother had to leave my sister behind in Hong Kong because she was not my father's daughter. She was only twelve years old. My mother spent the next three years becoming a Canadian citizen. She learned the names of the provinces, and their respective capitals, and the pledge of allegiance to the Union Jack. Unfortunately, none of it really sounded like English. Even at age seven, I realized that the *lo fons* wouldn't understand the sounds she made.

When my mother saw my sister at the airport, she became a new person. Her tiredness fell away and there was a lightness in her body. Tears streamed down her face, yet she smiled and smiled. She stretched out her arms and ran toward her daughter. They locked each other in a tight embrace. Then my sister released herself. As she looked me up and down, her first words were, "Your nose turns up too much, sort of like a pig." My mother smiled with embarrassment and brushed it aside. I swallowed a lump in my throat.

We spent that night in my Uncle Eddy's house. They lived like the *lo fons*. Uncle Eddy operated a restaurant. He didn't live upstairs from it. His family lived in a proper house with living and dining rooms. My Aunt Lena didn't have to work. My mother told me that before Aunt Lena arrived, Uncle Eddy bought her a dresser for the bedroom, and filled it with lingerie, body lotions, and perfumes. That evening my mother, my sister, and I slept on a pull-out couch in the living room. My mother slept in the middle, her arms entwined around my sister.

The next day we went home to Cheatley on a Gray Coach bus. My mother and my sister sat together. I sat across from them, beside a large *lo fon* woman. It was a long journey, and I watched, as my sister fell asleep, her head gently resting on Mother's shoulder, her lips slightly parted and letting out small puffs of air.

My father met us at the bus stop in Cheatley. It was a town of 2000 people, too small to have a real station. An unmarried brother and sister managed a candy store that also sold ice cream, magazines, comics, and bus tickets. Each carrying a piece of luggage, we began to walk the two blocks to my father's hand laundry.

We must have made an odd-looking sight as we walked along the sidewalk. My father was a tiny man, barely five feet tall. Wrinkles were deeply engraved into his face. He tensely knitted his eyebrows so that two deep furrows formed in the middle of his forehead and extended to the bridge of his nose. He wore an oversized brown herringbone wool coat that had been left in the laundry by one of the customers, and a peaked brown wool cap. His steps were short and close together as he struggled with the weight of my sister's brown leather suitcase, trying to keep it from dragging on the sidewalk. He remained several steps ahead of us. Even when unencumbered, my father never walked with his head up. His eyes were always fixed on the ground.

Behind him, the three of us persevered against the March wind with our heads tucked into our chests, protecting ourselves from the sprays of snow. I wrestled with my share of my sister's bags and tried to keep pace with my mother walking in the middle. But after bumping into her several times she suggested that I walk behind. Mother and I were dressed in old winter coats given to us by one of the ladies from the Presbyterian church. They were shapeless and hung loosely on both of us. Mine had a belt that was tightly buckled, forming a skirt with deep folds around my waist. I was expected to grow into it. My sister wore a blue wool coat, tailor-made in Hong Kong, as smart as the one worn by the doctor's young wife. Her one free hand clutched the lapels together to keep the wind off her chest. And the wind whipped in every direction the previously obedient strands of her freshly permed hair.

My father, my mother, and I were all small and dark. My mother was round-faced and plump, while my father and I were thin and wiry. We both had high cheekbones and skin that stretched tautly around slightly protruding jaws. My hands were like my father's. They were large, with joints that were thickly knuckled and square at the fingertips.

Walking with us, my sister was tall, elegant, and exquisite. We were coarse, tough, and sinuous. Her face was a perfect oval with ivory skin, the texture of flower petals. But it was her hands that always captured people's attention. The palms were narrow and the long slender fingers ended in nails that glistened like water drops. When she held them together they reminded me of tendrils on a vine, seeking and wrapping — vulnerable and treacherous.

We passed the hardware store, turned a corner and came to my father's laundry, our home. My father set down the suitcase he was carrying and lifted the wooden latch on the panelled wooden door, then opened the heavier wooden door, the one with the glass window, and let us into the first room of the laundry. Because it was winter, we were greeted by a blast of sulphurous air from the coal burning stoves. My sister gasped. My father lifted the hinged portion of the handmade wooden counter that separated the work area from the customers. He awkwardly stepped aside as we filed past him. Silently we watched as my mother's smile tightened and her eyes grew large with anxiety, while her older daughter surveyed and assessed.

My sister glanced at the wooden shelves, stacked with brown paper bundles of finished laundry. We walked past a wooden table, the top thickly swathed with old blankets and sheets. At the edge of the table stood an iron, and beside it, a basin of water with a bamboo whisk resting inside. She pointed to two long horizontal rollers that were held up by a wooden frame. I explained that this was an ironing press. When my father bought the laundry, it was considered a real bonus, a true labour-saving device. When it was turned on, wrinkled bedding, tablecloths, tea towels, and pillowcases were fed between the humming, rotating rollers. Like magic they piled on the shelf underneath in smooth folds like sheets of molten lava. On ironing days my father stood at these tables from early morning until late at night. At the end of the day he rubbed *Tiger Balm* into his aching muscles.

My mother held open the red and yellow paisley curtain that concealed the washing room. The first thing that caught my sister's attention was the washing machine. It stood in a drainage pan in the middle of the floor. It was a monstrous steel barrel, held up horizontally by four posts, looking like some mythical headless beast. Along one wall was a row of three wooden tubs. Attached to the one at the end was a hand-cranked mangle, used to wring out water. Inside one tub was a four-legged wooden stand with an enamel basin. Above it hung a clothesline between two nails. Dangling down were three thin hand towels and facecloths. My sister's eyes moved slowly about the room. She swallowed as she looked at the four burner coal stove with an oven. On the front burner was a large canning pot filled with hot water and holding a ladle. Beside the stove, on a wooden shelf covered in faded blue-and-white-checked oilcloth, was a two burner electric hotplate. The rings were finely cracked and the electric coils were recessed inside. In the corner, standing at attention, was a tall cylindrical water heater made of galvanized iron. Connected to it was a small coal burner. Hot water flowed from the taps only on washdays which were Mondays and Thursdays. Along the wall that led to the stairs were four straight-backed wooden chairs and a wooden table covered with the same faded, blue-checked oilcloth that was beneath the electric hotplate.

It seemed a long time before anyone spoke. Then I heard my mother's voice.

"Irene-*ah*, hang up Elder Sister's coat and take her upstairs. Show her where she'll sleep."

After I hung up both our coats, I led my sister past the faded wallpaper of large yellow pansies, up the wooden stairs, and past the window whose frame was stuffed with rolls of rags, keeping out the winter air. We stood on a floor covered with a piece of worn and finely cracked linoleum, patterned with brown and blue paisleys. My sister set her suitcase down beside her. I pointed to a bed behind us. "That's where Baba sleeps." Then I pointed to a narrow room off the main one. "You and Mah and I sleep in there." A single bed was jammed against the end wall; at a right angle stood a bunk bed. Across from the bunk was a four-pane window. A flowered-print curtain, threaded with a string, was tied to a nail in each top corner of the wooden frame. She walked over and poked her head in the doorway. "You can sleep on the bottom bunk; I sleep on the top." My sister stood in the doorway, listening. I touched the large wooden dresser that stood opposite from my father's bed. "This is where we keep our clothes. I use the bottom drawer. You can have the middle one. Baba and Mah use the small drawers at the top."

"Well, if that isn't enough room, I can keep the rest in my suitcase."

"Yeah," I said. "You can shove your suitcase under your bed."

The next day when I returned home from school, I saw the photographer from the local newspaper in front of the laundry. My sister was standing beside a drift of snow and the man was taking her picture. By the time she started school two days later, her picture had appeared on the front page of the town paper.

For the few months that were left in that school year, my sister was in the grade eight class. But the following September, after her sixteenth birthday, the school placed her in grade seven. We never walked to school together. I remember often seeing her at recess, alone in a corner of the schoolyard. Our schoolyard was separated from the train tracks by a high wire-mesh fence. My sister always watched the trains whistle by as I played and laughed and talked with my friends.

While my sister was in Hong Kong, we lived on a diet of soup made from chicken bones, salted fish and pork, and dried vegetables. When she arrived, there was suddenly meat on the chicken bones, and fresh fruit on the table. My mother cooked my sister's favourite dishes. Lily picked at the food and rejected her efforts. My mother watched in despair as her daughter's unhappiness grew and seeped into our lives like a persistent mist. Lily longed for her friends in Hong Kong. She told me stories about her life there. With each telling our town became more dull, our home more meagre, our food more plain, our clothes more shabby. Even her new Canadian name, Lily, so evocative of her delicate beauty, and given to her by our neighbour across the road, did little to make her feel more at home.

Several months after Lily arrived, Mother decided to take us to Toronto to visit Uncle Eddy and Aunt Lena. Uncle Eddy took us for *dim sum* at a restaurant in Chinatown. Afterwards we shopped for groceries in the China Trading Store. The atmosphere at the store was always dusty and mysterious. The mingled, conflicting odours from the many packages of dried fish, shrimps, oysters, scallops, and mushrooms had a pungency that prickled the nostrils. The China Trading Store had glass cases along one wall. Inside were dried roots, seeds, and herbs that were carefully weighed on a hand-held scale before they were wrapped in white paper and sold. There were barrels containing "thousand-year-old" eggs, and shelves of fresh fruit. On that particular day, there was displayed a small shipment of fresh lychees. No one in our family had had lychees since coming to Canada. My sister looked at them and touched them with her long white fingers. It was then that I noticed a man staring at us from a corner of the store. He was a tall, powerfully built man. His thick black hair was greased and combed straight back. He had a strong jaw and a nose that was slightly aquiline, unusual for a Chinese. His clothes were new and fashionable, his shoes black and polished. The other men in Chinatown were shabby, and their spirits were worn by living in the Gold Mountain. This man possessed a confidence that was enigmatic, predatory. His gaze fastened on my sister, and he watched as her hands picked up the lychees, and then put them back. My sister looked up and turned to meet his eyes. Then he suddenly walked toward us and shook hands with Uncle Eddy.

"Ah, Eddy, good to see you. How are you? How's business?"

"Not bad, not bad. And how about you, Tom?

"The usual. And who are these two beautiful girls?" the man asked as his gaze once again fixed upon my sister.

"Yes, these are my two nieces, Lily and Irene. This is their mother, Chung *Tai Tai*. I'd like you to meet Tom Leung." The man looked us over. Uncle Eddy went on proudly. "They're visiting the big city. Later this afternoon they're leaving on the bus for Cheatley."

Tom turned to my mother. "Cheatley, I'm going that way myself. I can give you a lift."

"Oh no. We don't want to take you out of your way. It would be too much trouble," protested my mother.

Tom wouldn't hear of it, and that afternoon he made the first of many visits to our home.

In 1955, Tom Leung was forty-seven years old and a very wealthy man. He owned several restaurants in Chinatown, three houses, and a fancy car. However, he was still unmarried. Unlike other Chinese men his age, he had never returned to China to look for a wife. He had come to Canada as a young boy. A self-educated man, he moved with ease in the white man's world. He spoke English perfectly and he read their newspapers. When he joked with the *lo fons*, he laughed like an equal, throwing his head back with his mouth wide open. Other Chinese always came to him when they needed someone to fill out forms, or to read and answer letters from the government. In Chinatown, this gave him special status — a sense of power. This air of confidence, along with his flashing eyes and quick laughter, were like a magnet. But along with this expansive, easy charm, there was a shark-like quality that seemed to devour people.

A week after our ride home in Tom's car, he came to visit us. He drove up in a shiny sea-green car with gleaming chrome bumpers and a wrap-around windshield. What impressed me most were his sunglasses. They were mirrors that rested on the bridge of his nose and reflected his world around him. What impressed my mother, though, were his gifts of food. He brought a barbecued duck, oranges, assorted *dim sum* from Chinatown, and lychees for Lily.

My mother was obviously flattered that a man with Tom's exalted reputation of wealth and influence should decide to visit us so soon.

"Ah, Leung *Sen Sun*, how are you? Come in. Come in. How good of you to come and visit. Sit down. Sit down."

"My pleasure. Now that we're all in *Gam Sun* we must stick together. I've brought some small gifts for your family."

"Oh, you needn't be so full of ceremony. Just come and visit."

"No trouble at all." Tom gave the bag of food to my mother, but first he took out the bag of lychees and handed them to my sister. Lily blushed, murmured thank you; she held Tom's gaze.

My father exchanged brief pleasantries with Tom and returned to work. Tom sat down on a wooden chair. Lily and I sat across from him. My mother placed the *dim sum* that Tom had bought on a plate, sliced some oranges, and filled a pot with water to boil for tea. I could tell by the way she fussed that she was embarrassed by the meagreness of our home. Tom looked at the unfinished plank floors, the dangling cords with the bare light bulbs, and the worn-out equipment for washing clothes. His eyes, though, always returned to rest on Lily's face.

Next Sunday, Tom visited our home again. Once more he offered gifts of steamed buns, barbecued meats, and fruit. But this time he had a stack of Chinese movie star magazines for Lily. "Here, these are for you, Lily."

"Ah, Leung *Sen Sun*, thank you so much. You have gone too far, too much trouble." Lily beamed and shyly accepted the gift. She told Tom that Hung Bo Bo was her favourite singer and her favourite actress, and that she always went to her movies in Hong Kong.

"Perhaps next week, I could come and take you and your sister to Chinatown to see the movies. Chung *Tai Tai*, would you like to come as well?"

"I won't be able to come. Too much work in the laundry. It's very kind of you to invite the girls. You really shouldn't go to such expense."

"Oh, Mah, it would be so much fun. I haven't seen a movie since I left Hong Kong. It's very kind of Leung *Sen Sun* to invite me and Irene." Lily leaned eagerly forward in her chair, her hands clasped together in her lap. I hadn't seen her so excited since she arrived. From the dark look she shot in my direction, I knew that my wishes were not a consideration.

"Well then, it's settled. Next Sunday I'll come and take the girls for lunch in Chinatown, and then to the movies." Tom sat back in his wooden chair and inhaled deeply on his cigarette. I watched the smoke come out of his mouth, curl upwards, slowly disappearing.

The next Sunday, Lily wore a blue-and white striped full-skirted dress with a collar that tied in a bow at the front, and black slip-on flats on her feet. I wore a red shirt-waist dress with a gathered skirt and ruffles around the collar, and black patent leather shoes with buckles. Lily waited eagerly; I was resigned. That afternoon I rode alone in the back seat of Tom's car. At the movies, my sister sat in the middle.

After that day's outing, Tom came to visit us every Sunday. As Sunday came closer, I sensed Lily's swelling excitement and anticipation. On Saturday night she washed her hair and slept in curlers. Sunday morning she woke up singing and smiling. By the time I returned from Sunday school, Tom was at our house, engaging Lily in conversation and laughter.

Over the next few months Tom bought our family many gifts. He bought Lily a record player and records of Chinese music. One day he even came with a television. Mother and Lily greeted these gifts with delight and enthusiasm. My father muttered indecipherable comments under his breath and carried on with his work, his eyes always on the floor.

One day I returned home from Sunday school and found Tom and Lily speaking very seriously to my parents. Tom was earnestly explaining as he leaned forward in his chair, "I wish to become Lily's godfather, her *kai yaah*. I could make life more comfortable for her and help towards her dowry when the time comes. As you know, I have no family of my own."

"Leung *Sook* is already like an uncle, another father. He comes every Sunday and has been so good to us," added Lily. Her face was radiant.

Mother was beaming, as if she couldn't believe the good fortune. "Leung *Sook*, you honour us with your proposal. We would welcome you as a member of our family."

My father mumbled agreement, as he sat perched uneasily at the edge of his stool. Tom rested comfortably back in his chair, one foot resting on the other knee. He smiled broadly and confidently as the smoke from his cigarette rose gently, vanishing into the air.

That evening over dinner, Tom, Lily, and Mother talked and laughed as they planned for a celebration banquet. My father and I quietly ate and exchanged glances.

After Lily and I went to bed that night, I woke up to the sound of loud voices. As Lily was softly, steadily breathing, I crept out of bed and crouched at the top of the stairs. I heard my father's voice.

"Something is not right. Tom is hiding his true feelings. They're not right. He's too close to her. I don't feel right about it."

My mother hissed back in a loud whisper. "Don't you see that he makes Lily happy? What can be wrong about his attention? He's old enough to be her father! She's just a teenager. He looks upon her as a daughter. Your suspicions are ridiculous."

"I don't know. It just doesn't feel right."

"Listen. He even said that he wants to be her godfather. You're just jealous that he's rich and successful! We should be honoured that he wants to help us. I'm not going to risk Lily's happiness. I'm going to bed." My mother turned sharply. As she started up the stairs, I dashed back into the bedroom and scurried under my covers.

And so Tom continued to embrace our lives with his lavish gifts. Arrangements were made for a celebration banquet, making Tom's entry into our family official and respectable. Friends from Chinatown were invited. Everyone could see that Tom Leung had become Lily's godfather, her *kai yaah*. Everyone could see that his feelings were honourable. Lily was luminous, like a bride, in the new red silk dress that Tom had chosen for her. He sat proudly beside her, the smoke from his cigarette languidly floating above their heads. Mother sat at the banquet table and looked triumphantly at my father. Any nagging anxieties had been obviously banished to the corners of her mind.

In the months that followed, my father's gaze rarely left the floor. We were drowning in Tom's beneficence. He installed a bathtub and sink in the washroom upstairs so that we no longer had to wash in the wooden laundry tubs. He bought us a refrigerator. He even constructed a small addition to our house. His visits began to last for several days, until he became a permanent guest in the addition that he had built. He even took Lily away on overnight weekend trips. One Sunday night, looking out the upstairs window, I saw Tom and Lily returning in Tom's car. Lily was asleep. Tom's arm was around her and he kissed her gently on the lips to wake her up. When I saw them get out of the car, I hurried into bed and pulled the covers over my head. I never mentioned to anyone what I saw.

The following Wednesday, I had a headache at school and the teacher let me come home early. I walked in the back door. My parents didn't know I was there. As I peeked around the door to the work area, I saw my father shove a letter in my mother's face.

"Read this. Read what Eddy's written. People are talking about your daughter and her *kai yaah*. You've got to do something about this." My father spat out the words *kai yaah* like bile stuck his throat.

As my mother silently read the letter she started to cry. "But Tom makes Lily happy. Life here has been so hard for her. She hasn't made any friends of her own. And he has spent so much money on us. What can we do?"

"Tom's feelings for Lily aren't those of a godfather. You know that. Stop fooling yourself. Do you want Lily to marry Tom?"

"You know what I want for my daughters. I don't want them to be like us. I want them to marry men, you know, educated, higher class. I want them to be Canadians. Not helpless, like us." My mother looked desperate. "Tom has been so good to us. How can we tell him to go?"

"Well, if this keeps up, the talk in Chinatown will grow; Lily will have no marriage prospects. And then what?"

My mother put the letter down on the ironing table, looked at my father as she wiped her face, turned and left the room. I tiptoed out of the house and crossed the road to call on a friend.

After that, the line of my mother's mouth changed. Her lips were pressed tightly together with the corners tucked in, and the two tendons in her neck stood out from her collar bone to her jaw. Her eyes, bewildered, became moist whenever she looked at Lily and Tom.

The quarrelling between my parents grew worse. And it was over little things. My father exploded one night because the soup wasn't hot enough.

"I've been working all day 'till I'm like a worn-out clog. And you can't even come up with hot soup!"

One humid summer evening, while Lily and Tom were out for a drive to escape the heat, my mother chased after my father as he ran into the backyard. She pleaded with him. "Tom has to leave this house. I know that now. But I can't bring myself to do it. You have to do it."

"But Lily is your daughter. You need to take charge."

"I can't. Don't you see. Lily hates me. She hates me because I left her in Hong Kong, even though I had no choice. If I make Tom leave she'll hate me even more. You have to tell Tom to leave, for my sake, for the sake of our family."

One afternoon in September, I returned home from school, went to my favourite corner and sat down on a squat wooden stool, opening a book of fairy tales I had borrowed from my teacher. The atmosphere felt different, clouds of tension and relief hanging in the air at the same time. My parents were silently working. My mother was preparing supper and my father was ironing clothes. A few minutes after I entered, Lily walked in. "Where's *kai yaab's* car? He's usually here by now." Before anyone spoke, Lily understood. Panic and fear radiated from her eyes. She dashed upstairs to the small room that Tom had added. She saw the bed and opened the empty drawers of the dresser.

Lily came hurtling down the stairs. Mother was standing at the kitchen table, slicing vegetables for supper. Lily, her body rigid, walked over and faced her. Rage emanated from every pore in her body. Her words were like knives, slashing the air around her. "Where is he? Why is his room empty?" In the silence that followed, I thought the air around us would explode. I wanted to fade into the flowered wallpaper, to become just a face, flat on the wall, staring out. Any movement would let them know I was there. I knew if I stayed perfectly still, I would become invisible.

Mother laid down the cleaver on its side, lifted her head and spoke. "He had to leave, Lily. He had to leave on business. He's opening a new restaurant up north somewhere."

Lily screamed, "You're lying. He didn't have to go. You made him." Her eyes shot toward my father. He stood in the adjoining ironing room with his back to her, pressing shirts, his arms moving like a robot's.

Mother implored, "Lily, you've got to try and understand. Tom agreed to go. He wants you to have a life of your own. He wants you to marry a Chinese boy, close to your own age, someone who's educated, so you can be a real Canadian." She reached into her apron pocket. "Here, he left a letter for you."

As Lily read Tom's letter, her disbelief gave way to tears. Then she walked into the ironing room, stopping a few feet from my father. Her rage and anguish rose from deep inside her, lacerating each of us. She glared at him as she spoke. "You're the one who told him to go. You're the one who made him leave. I *hate* you. I *hate* everything about you. I *hate* this laundry. The *lo fons* come in here with their dirty clothes and laugh behind your back. And all you do is smile."

My father carefully placed his iron on the table and turned, facing Lily as he spoke. "Lily, Lily, I know this is hard. But it is for the best. Even Tom knows this." He held out his arms toward her as he spoke. I could tell that he wanted to put them around her, but did not dare. Instead, she stood alone, covered her face with her hands, and wept, dropping Tom's letter on the floor. Mother walked over to her and lightly touched her shoulder. Lily immediately recoiled. My mother dropped her arm and took a step back. Lily stopped crying, straightened herself, and wiped her cheeks; staring all the while at my father and then our mother. Before my eyes my sister turned into stone; hard, cold, and impenetrable.

After that, I never saw Tom again. I don't know what happened to him. He never answered Lily's letters. I spent as much time away from home as possible. Any pleasures that I experienced with friends at school or at play, I hid when I came home. In the face of Lily's sorrow, I felt ashamed. What right had I to be happy? I grew more and more fearful of Lily.

A glass of spilt milk, or my laughing too loud, unleashed in her a torrent of rage. She never spoke to my father again. At first he tried to make amends. He bought food that she liked. When he tried to engage her in conversation she never answered. She always turned her face away. We became accustomed to the silence. An invisible shroud encircled each of us and separated our lives.

Three years later, my mother arranged a marriage between Lily and a young Chinese man, an accountant, only four years older. He was tall and hollow-chested. His cheeks were severely pock-marked, his smile too eager. I remembered Lily at her wedding ceremony. Her eyes were glazed. The "I do" was barely audible.

Afterwards at the reception, Lily sat, stone-faced, next to her husband at the head table. She watched the smoke from his cigarette coil slowly upwards, fading into the air.

2

THE GOLD MOUNTAIN COAT

THE SMALL TOWN THAT WAS MY HOME WAS TYPICAL OF many small towns in Ontario. It had one main street, one elementary school, one district high school, and five churches — Presbyterian, Anglican, United, Roman Catholic, and a Dutch Reform Church on the edge of town. Its distinctive architectural features were the funeral home and the post office. The funeral home was a beautiful white-washed brick mansion with immaculately manicured lawns and tidy flowering shrubs. It was close to the centre of the town and infused it with a gentle serenity. The post office was neatly built of red bricks. It had a steep roof and a clock tower that rose up like a church spire. And it chimed every hour.

The main street of our small town had a dime store that sold everything from *Evening in Paris* perfume to stationery and hammers. It also had a clothing store, a jewellery shop, a hardware store, a drugstore, a barber shop, and a restaurant that served Canadian food. And, typical of all small towns, it also had a Chinese restaurant and a Chinese hand laundry.

My father operated the hand laundry and the other Chinese family managed the Chinese restaurant. I was the only Chinese child in the town. When my family first arrived, the restaurant was run by two brothers and their father, Sam Sing. The entrance of the restaurant was flanked by projecting glass windows. Just inside the windows on a shelf were several large dusty-leafed sansevierias. The floors were covered with old-fashioned black and red lino tiles laid out in a diamond checkerboard pattern. There was a shiny speckled Formica counter with stools of circular seats uphol-stered in vinyl, and rimmed with a wide band of shiny chrome. Along one wall was a counter with built-in stainless steel sinks for washing glasses. Above was a shelf where the soft drink, soda, and sundae glasses were all neatly arranged in rows, according to size. Beside this was an ancient cooler with glass sliding doors that housed the milk, cream pies, and miniature china coffee creamers. But what I remembered most were the booths with the wooden seats and straight hard backs. Whenever I sat in one of these booths, I felt as if I had entered a little wooden room surrounded by brown grainy walls. There hung from the ceiling, a huge four-blade fan, that in the summer hovered and whirred — a huge hum-ming dragonfly.

The proprietor, Sam Sing, stood behind the counter of his restaurant. He was a tall, straight-backed, grim-looking man with deep wrinkles cross-hatching his face. Sam rarely smiled, but when he did he showed a set of gold teeth that matched his gold-rimmed glasses. He rarely spoke, but when he did his voice had the raspy quality of sandpapers rubbing together.

There was nothing ingratiating about Sam. He glared at his customers from behind his glasses. In his presence, I was always struck speechless. I was afraid to return his gaze; I felt diminished and insignificant.

When I first met Sam Sing, he was already in his seventies; he had a head of thick, almost totally black hair parted at the side. He seemed robust and alert, and for a man his age he moved with amazing agility. My parents told me that Sam owed his exceptionally good health to drinking medicinal turtle soup made with *Gilbey's* gin. According to local legend, whenever Sam felt unwell, he asked a couple of local teenage boys to catch him a turtle from the nearby creek. The two boys arrived through the back door of the kitchen with a bulging burlap bag. Once, when I was in the dining room, I saw Sam give the boys a silver fifty-cent piece each from the cash register. The freckle-faced boys looked at each other and giggled, then left, clutching their coins. Sam stared after them, his eyes dark with contempt. I just barely heard the "hrump" he let out under his breath as he shut the money drawer. The older son walked into the dining room and as the wooden door swung away to and fro behind him, I caught a glimpse into the kitchen. The younger son held a cleaver over his head, poised to come crashing down on the squirming, unsuspecting, overturned turtle. The pieces of turtle meat were tossed into a large pot of water along with medicinal herbs, preserved roots, and dried gecko lizard. Then followed hours of simmering to produce a clear, brown, pungent, tonic soup.

Because of their work in the restaurant, Sam and his sons smelled faintly of cooking oil, in the same way, I suppose, that my father smelled of soap. Sam and his sons dressed alike. They wore white cotton shirts with the sleeves rolled up to their elbows and baggy black pants. And each wore a flat white half-apron tied around his waist.

Sam was proud of the fact that he had fathered two sons who would carry on his business and his family name. In contrast to Sam's stern, imposing demeanour, his sons were round-faced, smooth-skinned, and smiling. They reminded me of bookends; they looked almost identical, except that one was very fair-skinned, while the other was very dark. Ken, the younger son looked after the kitchen, where he cooked French fries, hot beef and hot chicken sandwiches, fluorescent red sweet and sour chicken balls, and assorted chop sueys. John, the older son, spent his days rushing back and forth through the swinging wooden doors that separated the dining room from the kitchen, reporting customers' orders, and then cheerfully carrying out their dishes.

John always greeted the restaurant guests enthusiastically. He smiled and gushed in his broken English. Sam Sing spoke only when the customers lined up at the cash register, and then it was to blurt out the price of their meal. John often seemed embarrassed by his father's gruffness; there was an unspoken apology in his own exceptional friendliness.

The brothers were kind to me. I remember visiting the restaurant and frequently coming out with a double-scooped ice cream cone. Often the brothers came to visit my parents in the afternoon, during the quiet time between the lunch and supper hours in the restaurant. But Sam Sing never entered our house. His enterprise was prosperous, whereas ours was poor. Did he feel that we were beneath him? Or was it that we reminded him of earlier and more meagre times that were best forgotten?

I looked forward to the visits by John and Ken. They took a special older-brotherly interest in me. When one of them came to our laundry, he often brought me a special treat, such as an *Oh Henry* or *Sweet Marie* chocolate bar. These were always shyly, but enthusiastically welcomed, for my parents could not afford such luxuries.

What I remember most about Ken and John, though, was that in the winter they visited our house one at a time. Between them, they shared a single coat. It was a shapeless, black, wool garment. The pile was completely worn, the sleeves were permanently accordioned, the buttons were all mismatched, and the corners of the collar curled upwards. Occasionally, when the weather was not too severe, one brother would arrive at the laundry dressed in the coat. A half hour or so later the other brother would dash over wearing just a thin sweater over his white shirt. This made my mother laugh and she teased them about their excessive thrift.

For many years, Sam Sing and his sons lived contentedly in this bachelor existence. The sons each had a clearly defined role in the running of the restaurant and Sam presided over everything. Ken had come to Canada unmarried, but John had left his wife, son, and daughter back in China. After working through government channels for several years, John was finally given permission to bring his family over.

My mother often helped John compose his letters back to China. Whenever he received mail from home, he rushed over to share it with my parents. One day he showed me a picture, taken in a studio, of his wife, son, and daughter. The wife and daughter had freshly permed hairstyles parted at the side, revealing high broad foreheads. The son was dressed in too-large overalls, the bib almost touching his chin. The mother was sitting down with her hand resting on her son's shoulder, while the daughter, who was a few years older, stood slightly but noticeably apart. I looked at this picture and felt the solemnity of their stares. It seemed strange to me that John was really the father. His youth and exuberance were in such contrast to the personality of my own father, who was over sixty when I was born. My mother was pleased that I would at last have Chinese playmates. Although both my parents were proud that I had learned English so quickly, I knew they were concerned that I was becoming "too Canadian." John told me that I would be in charge of teaching his children English and taking them to school. As he spoke, the brown in his eyes took on a liquid quality and his eyebrows were arched so that dark vertical furrows appeared between them. Once more, I looked at the children in the photograph. Then I looked at John. Did he expect me to be friends with them? I was the only Chinese child in the town and since coming to Canada I had only played with *lo fon* children. Did these children from China know about *Howdy Doody* and *Captain Kangaroo?* What would I have to teach them besides English? I began to feel a weight on my chest.

When an arrival date for John's family was established, Sam permitted his sons to close the restaurant for a half-day. Both brothers were to go to the airport to greet the family from China. The brothers recognized their father's generosity in giving them a half-day off. For five years, the restaurant had never been closed. However, there was one problem. It was winter and they had only the one coat to share between them. Both John and Ken realized that a new coat was a significant purchase, one that would have to have Sam's approval. As the arrival date of John's family drew nearer, and the temperatures grew colder, the need for a second coat was becoming urgent.

John and Ken discussed the purchase of a second coat from every angle. How could they convince the old man to part with enough money for a new coat? Timing was essential. After closing time, Ken and John always scurried around the restaurant. They swept and washed the floors, filled the glass sugar dispensers and the miniature china creamers, and cleaned up the dirty dishes. Meanwhile, Sam sat alone in the wooden booth at back of the restaurant. He carefully calculated the day's profits, his fingers flying over the rings of a black wooden abacus brought many years ago from China. If the earnings were good, Sam invited his sons to share a glass of whisky. But if the earnings were poor, Sam drank alone and glowered at the wooden walls of the booth while his sons continued silently working. Naturally, John and Ken decided to approach Sam on a night the whisky was shared.

The day after his discussion with Ken, John came to visit my parents. Though I heard him chuckling as he confided to my mother about the logistics of the timing, every word was coated with resentment. At first he decided that Saturday should be the asking day. But then my mother pointed out that if permission to purchase was granted on a Saturday night, Sam might change his mind by the time stores opened on Monday. She convinced John that Friday was a better day. Business was usually good. And the stores were open on Saturday.

On the chosen Friday, John visited us late in the afternoon. The wind sounded particularly shrill that day as it sprayed blasts of white powdery snow over the sidewalks. When John walked into the laundry, he looked as if someone had dusted him with icing sugar. He seemed quite agitated. I remember hearing him speak with great determination. "In a few days my family will be here. We'll all be living upstairs. I will be the one responsible for them." He glanced at my mother who nodded in agreement. "I'm going to have to stand up to that old man. I carry all this money in my pocket." He patted the front pocket of his pants emphatically before continuing. "And I have to ask permission to spend it. What right does he have to object? I work hard. This isn't China. Things are different here." Again, my parents said very little. They mostly smiled and nodded reassuringly. Then John suddenly remembered, "Today is payday at the mill!" He smiled and exclaimed, "Today business will be good. Guaranteed!"

Just before he left, John walked over to the corner where I sat pretending to read a comic book. He patted me on the shoulder and grinned. "Not too much longer now." I looked up and smiled. John looked so happy. As I nodded, I felt an ever so slight cramp in my stomach.

That Friday, after the restaurant closed, Sam counted his money, smiled, and invited his sons for a glass of whisky. This was the moment John had been waiting for. His father offered him a glass. He took a large, quick gulp. "Father, you know that my wife and family will be arriving on Wednesday. You have been generous enough to let Ken come with me to the airport to greet them." Sam nodded his head.

John continued, with Ken nervously looking on. "But, Father, we have only one coat. The weather is very cold. We need to buy another coat."

Sam carefully set down his whisky glass. His face slowly hardened at the boldness of his son's request. John was ready to panic, but then Ken blurted out, "John's son will need a coat for school. Your grandson cannot walk to school without a coat. A second one for us, one the boy can grow into."

Sam's face broke into a smile. His gold teeth gleamed. "Very good," he said and finished his whisky. The brothers breathed a sigh of relief.

The next morning, John and Ken dashed across the street to the clothing store that was owned by Paul Holmes. Paul had arrived in the small town from Europe just after the Second World War. Like Sam Sing, he saw opportunities for a new life in the New World. He had been in business for only a few years when Sam Sing, having purchased the restaurant from its previous owner, arrived with his sons. Like Sam and his sons, Paul had worked hard building his business. And like them, he owed his present financial security more to self-denial and hard work, than to astute business sense. Over the years, Sam and his sons had bought the occasional piece of clothing from Paul, and Paul had eaten the occasional meal in the restaurant. Although everyone kept pretty much to themselves, they had a mutual respect that arose from a recognition of each other's hardships, honesty, and frugality.

John and Ken looked carefully around the store. Dark suits hung sombrely on racks, and shirts wrapped in plastic were stacked inside a case of wooden shelves. A cabinet with a glass counter and sides contained more shirts, sweaters, cuff links, and tie clips. Everything had a place. The air smelled faintly of sizing. The brothers suddenly became acutely aware of the shabbiness of their own clothing and the dim scent of cooking oil emanating from their pores. Paul smiled politely at them. And they smiled politely back. Finally John said to Paul, "My wife, my boy, and my girl come to Canada from

China. We want a coat."

Paul showed John and Ken many coats — grey ones, blues ones, brown ones, double breasted, single breasted, with belts, without belts, but none would do. As John's fingers gently touched the thick pile of one coat and the borg fur collar of another, he realized without even being told that each was too expensive. Ken pointed out the price of one coat: It was twenty dollars! John sucked his breath between his teeth, making a whistling sound, to show his shock. At the restaurant a cup of coffee was ten cents, and a full meal of fish and chips with soup and dessert was fifty cents. How many would they have to sell, to pay for even the cheapest coat which was twelve dollars?

The brothers were both extremely frugal and not at all concerned with personal adornment or style.

Then Paul had an idea. He went into the storage closet at the back of the store. In contrast to the showroom where every item of clothing knew its place, the storage was crammed with outdated garments that Paul brought out twice a year to sell at reduced prices. He brought out a brown and orange plaid coat, covered in plastic. It was definitely not in style but, it was brand new. He offered it to the brothers for half the price of the cheapest coat in the store. That meant it was only six dollars. This was a bargain the brothers could not refuse. Ken tried it on. He admired himself in the full-length mirror. The coat was slightly too large. But no matter — the price was right. John turned to Paul. "Okay. We take." John reached into his pocket and brought out a thick wad of bills. He carefully handed Paul a blue five-dollar bill, and a green one-dollar bill.

Just as they were about leave the store, Paul shouted,

"Wait!" He quickly returned to his storage room and brought out another coat in dusty plastic wrap. John could tell that underneath the wrap the coat was a brownish grey tweed with large red flecks. With a twinkle in his eye, Paul cried, "One dollar." The brothers couldn't believe their luck! They didn't even bother to try on the coat.

After the purchase, John immediately hurried over to our laundry. My mother sat on a stool sorting socks for the wash, as John chuckled and bragged about their triumph. We heard every detail. Sam had apparently only grumbled a little about their over spending. But John knew that he was secretly impressed with the bargain they had struck with Paul. As John left, he reminded me, his voice nervous and happy with anticipation, "In another few days there will be Chinese children for you to play with." I nodded and smiled stiffly.

Four days later as I was walking home from school for lunch, I saw John and Ken waiting in line, outside the five-and-dime store, to board the bus to Toronto. Their coats were large and stiff, the shoulders too wide and the length too long. They reminded me of turtles with their heads poking through hard protective shells, one decorated in a brown and orange plaid, the other in dark grey with large red flecks. From the way they looked at the other passengers — the large heavy woman whose girth strained against the buttons of her faded wool jacket, and the young woman who stood slightly shivering in her thin fashionable coat and fur-trimmed ankle boots — I could tell that John and Ken were proud of their coverings, proof of the success they were experiencing in the Gold Mountain, decent shells for the old, shabby clothes hiding underneath.

I stood and waved to them. They smiled proudly back. In a few more hours there would be three more Chinese people in our small town. I would have to take the new children to school with me, introduce them to the teachers and to my friends. Translate for them, and more. I waved for a moment longer, then turned and ran all the way home.

3

EAT BITTER

HUA FAN STOOD IN FRONT OF THE IRONING TABLE LOOKING at the letter. He did not expect another from China so soon. The last one had arrived just two weeks earlier. He looked at the envelope, admiring the graceful, careful script that belonged to the village schoolmaster. As Hua Fan read, a mixture of real concern and guilty relief washed over him. His mother was seriously ill; he should return to China as soon as possible. He had waited five years for this opportunity, for an excuse to go back. With the war over, it would be safe. But how to tell Elder Uncle? Elder Uncle, who had provided passage on the boat, who had given him a home for the last five years, who was providing an opportunity to make money in *Gam Sun*, the Gold Mountain?

Hua Fan carefully refolded the letter and slipped it back inside the envelope. After putting it away underneath the wooden drawer holding the customer cash, he turned to the ironing table. There was one more shirt to iron for "Doctor Uncle." When Hua Fan was finished, he stacked it with the other pressed shirts and placed the handkerchiefs and collars on top. Then he wrapped the package of laundry in brown paper and tied it with string. As he was placing it on the wooden shelf along with the other parcels, a *lo fon* walked into the laundry. Hua Fan turned. Just as the door was closing, he caught a glimpse of the budding leaves on the tree outside the laundry. Standing behind the counter was a new *lo fon* uncle, one he didn't recognize. Hua Fan smiled at him, but before he was able to speak, the *lo fon* shouted, "Hey, Charlie, I've lost my ticket. I know — no tickee, no laundree." Hua Fan didn't even wait for the wild gesticulations to begin. After listening to a quick description of the items, he started to search for a tag with a listing that matched. Today he was lucky. He had to unwrap only three different bundles before the *lo fon* stranger recognized the one belonging to him. Some days, after a *lo fon* with no ticket left, he was stuck with as many as eight parcels to rewrap. Hua Fan cursed under his breath as he watch the *lo fon* step out the door, whistling, the package under his arm.

One week after his arrival in *Gam Sun*, Elder Uncle had sent Hua Fan to Doctor Uncle's house to pick up some laundry. The doctor's wife was a plump gentle woman who taught Sunday school at the Methodist church. She opened the door to the kitchen and motioned for Hua Fan to step inside, smiling as she spoke; warm, indecipherable sounds coming out of her mouth, a faint scent of flowery talc emanating from her clothes. She gestured to a chair and Hua Fan sat down. Before leaving the room to gather the clothes, she gave him a slice of cake on a thin china plate. The cake was moist and delicious, but the coating was sticky and sweet, leaving a dull ache in his teeth.

As Hua Fan trudged along with the bag of soiled laundry slung across his back, he stopped for a moment and stood looking around. The sky was a clear, chilling blue. He looked up and squinted at the sun. All around him the village was draped in white. Behind was a trail of footprints, each one like a shaft sliced deeply into the snow. The whiteness of the landscape felt eternal. It was hard to imagine what lay hidden underneath. Would the trees' grey branches, sticking out like bony gnarled fingers, really sprout green leaves? Was the soil under the snow really brown?

Hua Fan looked deceptively stocky. The many layers of stockings, pants, undershirts and sweaters under his thick black quilted cotton jacket created an impression of bulk. On his head he wore a brown knitted toque. His long black queue flowed from underneath his hat and down his back. Still, he never felt sufficiently protected from the winter air. It always managed to pierce, one by one, each stratum of clothing. Back in China, he had listened in disbelief to stories about the frigid temperatures in Canada. He laughed when he heard about men losing their ears and fingers after they were frozen. He had pictured them falling cleanly off, making a clink as they hit the ground! Every time he stepped out of the laundry he was shocked by the biting winter air. Even though he felt it every day, this Canadian winter would always be a mystery to him. They would never be on familiar terms.

As Hua Fan struggled through the foot-deep snow, something came hurtling out of nowhere and struck him on the mouth. His top lip started to swell and his teeth felt bruised as he watched the drops of blood fall one by one. The dark centres radiated and faded into the absorbing snow. Red on white. His blood tasted salty and metallic. When Hua Fan looked up he saw a pair of blue eyes, as cold as the surrounding air, menacing in their clarity, disconnected from face or body. He looked down again and saw, lying at his feet, a jagged chunk of ice. Suddenly the blue eyes creased into a laugh, and more chunks of ice and balls of snow were hurled at him.

"Chinky Chinky Chinaman sittin' on a fence. Tryin' t' make a dollar outa fifteen cents."

Hua Fan felt a rush of blood to his face as he fought the impulse to pick up the ice and throw it, smash it, into the offending face. Instead he clenched his teeth, pulled his chin into his chest, and ran to the safety of his uncle's laundry, with the image of those blue eyes forever burned into his memory.

That night, Hua Fan stood in front of the single, tiny, splotchy mirror in the laundry. He turned his head and looked at the thick black queue that hung like a snake down his back. He clutched the braid with his left hand and held a pair of scissors in his right. With his eyes tightly shut and his jaw clenched, he cut it off. Then he opened his eyes and looked at his reflection. From the front he looked no different. His hair was still held in place at the nape of the neck by the initial twist of the braid. With one hand he loosened it and watched it fall, framing the sides of his face. He wrapped his braid with a piece of brown paper and stuffed it inside his bamboo suitcase. This cold distant country was not his home. One day he would return to China. And he would be rich.

Hua Fan's gaze swept around the room where he now slept and worked. One month ago he had left China, his village in Hoi Ping county. If he closed his eyes he still saw the teahouse where he had worked as a servant. He felt the steam and smelled the fire and heard the bosses with their loud berating voices. The memories of being whipped and beaten remained fresh in his mind. He could still feel across his blistered shoulders the weight of the heavy pails of water dangling from the ends of a bamboo pole. His only moments of peace came when he swept the ashes in the bake ovens. Curling his body to make himself small and unobtrusive, he listened to the waiters tell the cooks stories about *Gam Sun*, the Gold Mountain, about how even the poorest man could become rich.

The day the letter from Elder Uncle in *Gam Sun* arrived, Hua Fan knew his luck had changed. Elder Uncle's only son had died the year before. If Hua Fan agreed to work for Elder Uncle in his hand laundry in the Gold Mountain, he would sponsor him as a paper son. Elder Uncle would even pay the $500 head tax. Of course, Hua Fan would eventually have to pay him back.

Hua Fan had heard from the men who returned from *Gam Sun* that life there could be gruelling and lonely. Old Lee with the crooked back, the number two cook, used to torment him when he caught Hua Fan dreaming. "Dreaming about *Gam Sun*, again, are you? How are you ever going to get there. Even if you did, you'd never last. *Eiyah!* Look how scrawny you are, like a dried-up piece of *bak choy!*"

Hua Fan never dared reply. But he thought to himself, "What could be worse than this?" He saw how the "guests" from the Gold Mountain behaved when they returned. People were always gathered around them. Their pockets were never empty. The waiters, with grins fixed on their faces, milled about like ants, attending to every need.

When the letter from Elder Uncle had arrived, the jeers

from Old Lee had stopped. He occasionally even smiled at Hua Fan. If Hua Fan wasn't mistaken, there were times when he seemed even humble.

One year later, Hua Fan boarded the large steamship that carried him and dozens of other Chinamen across the Pacific to *Gam Sun*. A tall, pale-faced man with strange orange hair loomed over them, herding the crowd in the right direction. He shouted at them in an odd-sounding language and yanked their long black queues when he wanted their attention. Hua Fan couldn't stop staring. He had never seen a person with so much hair on his face.

For twenty-two days, Hua Fan lived with other Chinamen at the bottom of the boat. Some of the men were returning for the second or third time. A few of them teased him as they looked him up and down. "What's a skinny fellow like you going to do over there? You think the streets are paved with gold? The *lo fons* treat their dogs better than a Chinaman." But he ignored their taunts. He never complained about the terrible food, the tossing of the ocean, or the mingling stench of unwashed bodies and vomit. Some of the boat uncles though were kind and a few of them taught him how to count to ten in English, to say "yes" and "no," "how much" and "thank you."

When the ship docked in the harbour at Salt Water City, most of the Chinamen stayed there. It was a bustling town, and already the Chinese had established a community. But Hua Fan had to go to the middle of the country, to a small town in northern Ontario, where his uncle operated a small hand laundry.

Hua Fan stood looking out the window of the train. Inside his coat pocket was a piece of brown paper with the name of his destination, Sydney. "Sit-nee," he whispered to himself. Just being able to pronounce it gave him comfort.

One of the boat uncles sat next to him on the train. Hua Fan was relieved that he would not have to travel alone across the country. Over the next few days, he watched as the scenery changed from looming rugged mountains to land flat as a table top. He listened to the boat uncle talk about his life in China, his wife and concubine, his servants, his mansion, his property. About his big business in *Gam Sun*, his big restaurant, many workers, big money. "Hua Fan, if you need a job, just come and see me." The boat uncle was dressed in a fine wool suit like the ones worn by the *lo fons*. He wore his hair cut short in the Western style. But Hua Fan noticed that although the cut of the coat was refined and elegant, his hands were thick and calloused.

When the train stopped in Winnipeg, the boat uncle left, again reminding Hua Fan what to do if he ever needed work. Shortly afterwards the scenery changed again, from flat land to thick coniferous forests on high rocky land. Hua Fan was sleeping when the train conductor shook him awake. "Hey, Charlie! This is your stop. Syd-nee."

He took out the piece of paper from his inside pocket and held it up. "Yes, this is it. SYD-NEE," shouted the conductor, nodding vigorously. Hua Fan stood, picked up his bamboo suitcase, and left the warmth of the train. As he stepped into the piercing cold January air, his breath looked like a cloud of smoke in front of his face.

Elder Uncle was a short, well-muscled man. His hands were large and rough, hanging well below his sleeves. His face was round like the sun, with slits for eyes that narrowed into creases when he smiled. He waited in an unobtrusive spot with his back against a pillar, staying clear of the *lo fons* who milled confidently about on the platform. His neck craned as he looked for his nephew. Although they had not seen each other for many years, they recognized each other immediately. In a sea of white faces, theirs were the only brown ones.

Sydney was a small lumber town in northern Ontario. In the summer it was hot, humid and infested with clouds of relentless blackflies. In the winter the snow gave the landscape a haunting, pristine beauty, but the temperatures were unbearable and unforgiving. It was a small town populated by a few families, but mostly by single men who worked for the lumber mill and who went into the lumber camps — single men who needed someone to wash their clothes.

Elder Uncle's laundry was on the first floor of a rundown frame building, a few blocks from the railroad tracks. Hua Fan looked up and saw a wooden sign above the doorway. Against a red background, the white letters said Lee Tang Hand Laundry. Elder Uncle unlocked the wooden door and Hua Fan stepped inside. His eyes took a few moments to get used to the dim light. Just inside the door was the handmade wooden counter that would separate Hua Fan and Elder Uncle from the customers when the business was open. On the other side of the counter was a wall lined with wooden shelves on which there were neatly stacked packages of finished laundry wrapped in brown paper. Along another wall were two "ironing beds," each a roughly made wooden table covered with old blankets, topped with an old sheet — all tightly tucked under the wooden surface and secured with nails. Elder Uncle walked past the brown-papered bundles and pushed aside a heavy green and red flowered curtain that divided the customer area from the washing section. In the middle of the floor was a monstrous looking washing machine. It was a massive grey metal barrel. Nestling inside was a similar-shaped wooden container punctured with holes the size of quarters. Carved into one side of both barrels were hinged doors where laundry was stuffed and removed. Hua Fan looked at the contraption, thinking that it resembled a giant insect with four metal legs standing inside a large metal pan with a drainage hole. To one side were three wooden laundry basins used for rinsing the clothes. A hand-cranked wringer was attached to the last basin and a tall stack of brown bamboo laundry hampers stood in the corner. Along another wall was a coal-burning stove for cooking and heating. Beside it stood the boiler. Hua Fan noticed a small bedroom off to one side. Inside were two narrow cots made of metal.

On that first evening in Sydney, Elder Uncle took Hua Fan's bamboo suitcase and shoved it under one of the beds. Then he turned to Hua Fan. "You've had a long journey. You rest a little while I get us something to eat. Tomorrow you will work."

Hua Fan nodded. He took off his coat and shoes, then lay down on the bed. The blankets were scratchy, but the mattress was soft, unlike the flat woven bamboo mats at home. He looked around, trying to make sense of his new surroundings and immediately fell asleep.

"Time to eat!" called Elder Uncle. Hua Fan roused himself, and walked to the square wooden table where he sat down on a stool. Supper was steamed white rice, chopped salted pork and egg, and soup from dried *bak choy*. Hua Fan ate eagerly and quickly, relishing the warmth and flavours of the food.

When Elder Uncle spoke, Hua Fan suddenly became aware of the the lack of conversation. He asked Hua Fan about the family back home and about the boat trip. Then Elder Uncle said very suddenly, "Tomorrow morning we will have to get up early. Wednesdays and Saturdays we sort the *lo fon*'s clothing. Mondays and Thursdays we wash. Tuesdays and Fridays we iron."

The next day, Hua Fan watched as a tall man with a large hooked nose like a mountain in the middle of his face, walked into the laundry. The stranger spoke to Elder Uncle in a loud voice. Elder Uncle smiled and nodded as he accepted a bundle of clothing. After the *lo fon* left, he carefully wrote in black ink with a tiny brush inside the collar of the shirt.

"Why are you doing that?" asked Hua Fan. He noticed the sly smile on Elder Uncle's face.

"I have to write their names in their shirts so I can give them back to the right people."

"They have Chinese names?"

Elder Uncle shook his head. "Come and look." Hua Fan nodded and grinned when he saw what was written: "Big Nose Uncle."

"I don't know what their names are," Elder Uncle said. "They don't know mine either. But I give them names. That one's Big Nose. There's Crooked Mouth Uncle, Doctor Uncle, Banker Uncle. They're no trouble. But some are terrible, like Drunk Uncle. But the worse is Shitty Pants Uncle. Never mind, though, as long as they pay."

Elder Uncle showed Hua Fan the giant bamboo basket

filled with white shirts. The arms of several shirts dangled
carelessly over the brim. He placed two squat, wooden stools
beside the basket and motioned Hua Fan to sit down next to
him.

"Take the collars off the shirts. They have to be washed
separately and then starched. All the socks have to be turned
inside out. Start with the socks."

Hua Fan laughed as he held a shirt in front of himself.
The tails dangled past his knees. "These lo fons are huge,
Elder Uncle. Look at the size of these shirts. I wonder if their
dicks are big too...." He shot Elder Uncle a sideways glance
and noticed the old man chuckling.

"Don't know. We don't get any closer than their underwear."

"And the lo fons have strange smells, Elder Uncle. They
must sweat a lot. Some of the socks are still damp. And the
ones that are dry are stiff."

"Well, Hua Fan, it's because of the strange food they
eat."

"Oh?"

"The lo fons eat a lot of something called cheese. It
stinks and has a taste that is even worse. It coats your mouth
and you can't get rid of the taste."

"Have you ever tried it?"

"Only once. I thought I would throw up." Elder Uncle
chuckled and shook his head. Hua Fan handled the socks
gingerly. He picked them up with his thumb and index fingers. He was barely able to put his hand inside the first sock
to turn it inside out. The acrid odour assaulted his nostrils
and left him gasping for air. Elder Uncle's hands, however,
were indifferent. They worked with a kind of mechanical

speed, while the corners of his mouth were turned down in an expression of concentration.

"Hua Fan, you have to work faster. Never mind, you will get used to the smell, I tell you. Today is not so bad. Sorting is the easy day."

Elder Uncle was right. Compared to the other tasks, sorting was painless. The next day, mounds of laundry were placed inside the wooden barrel washing machine. The barrel was rocked back and forth to agitate the clothes inside. Afterwards they were pulled out and submerged in the wooden tubs filled with icy water. The rinsing was repeated until there was no trace of soap. Then the clothes were cranked by hand through a wringer. The collars were washed separately and soaked in pails of starch. Handkerchiefs were boiled to loosen the dried snot that floated to the top of the pot like a film of pale green algae.

Because it was winter, a room at the back of the building was closed off. In a corner was a large cast-iron stove. It was filled with coal and the room was heated to about eighty degrees. Hua Fan looked up and saw parallel lines strung from one wall to the other about a foot from the ceiling. Elder Uncle worked steadily, reaching for wet laundry in the bamboo basket, then stepping up on a wooden stool and pegging it to the lines. As Hua Fan helped, the perspiration dripped down his face and back. When they could no longer bear the heat and the humidity, Elder Uncle opened the back door to release clouds of steam. But the door was quickly shut. Losing heat was losing money. When everything was dried, each article was rolled into a tidy package, placed in a bamboo hamper ready to be ironed the next day. By the end of his first washday, every muscle in Hua Fan's body ached and his hands and arms were raw and numb from being immersed in cold water.

Hua Fan watched the *lo fon* stranger leave, the brown package tucked at a cocky angle under his arm. As soon as the door closed, he spat into an enamel spittoon in the corner of the room. Then he picked up the iron and slammed it on the surface of the ironing table. He took a deep breath as he pushed back the memories of humiliation that now covered him like a coat of slime. The blow of ice against his mouth, drops of blood on snow. The memory of those blue eyes filling him with anger again and again. He dreaded walking into town, hearing those strange sounding words, taunting, full of hate — *Ching, Ching, China-man.* He was sick of always ingratiating himself to these white devils. Again he reminded himself. *This is not my real life.* In his mind he saw himself back in the village, dressed like a gentleman in fine clothes as he presided over the operations of his teahouse, chatting with a few select customers, amazing them with stories about the Gold Mountain, laughing as he told them about the *lo fons* — the big nosed hairy giants. Yes! It was true that their hair grew not only in different colours, but all over their bodies and half their faces.

Hua Fan thought about the letter from the village schoolmaster. He thought about his sick mother. He knew that Elder Uncle would be asking for news. He sucked in the right corner of his mouth. How to tell Elder Uncle that he would be leaving. How could he tell without seeming ungrateful?

He reached under the counter and pulled out a sack of

laundry and emptied it on the floor. Squatting beside the pile, Hua Fan saw how mechanically his hands sorted the soiled clothing, indifferently picking up dirty socks and underwear. He no longer even noticed the smells. When he finished he stood and stretched, then walked over to the ironing table. A quick glance at the basket filled with rolls of wrinkled laundry told him that they should be finished by two the next morning. He absent-mindedly picked up a shirt from the basket. He blew into the spray can and cast a fine mist over the shirt. Then he picked up an iron from the pot-bellied stove, pressed it on the table and checked the heat with the palm of his hand. Hua Fan chuckled silently to himself as he remembered the first time Elder Uncle showed him how to iron the *lo fons'* shirts. First the cuffs and sleeves, then the shoulders, last the body. But it was the folding that had seemed the most mysterious. Although Elder Uncle's fingers were thick and calloused, they moved as quickly and deftly as a magician's. Suddenly the shirt was a tidy rectangular package with the front tabs overlapping and the buttons straight down the middle. It had taken Hua Fan several weeks to be able to duplicate the result, with half the speed.

Elder Uncle opened the back door, letting a rush of spring air into the laundry. He poked his head inside and called excitedly, "Hua Fan, Hua Fan, come outside and look." Hua Fan stood the iron in an upright position and walked into the backyard.

Elder Uncle was crouching in the garden, examining the seedlings. He loved the garden. As soon as the snow started to melt, he looked forward to the ground warming up, then turning over the soil. After he finished digging, Elder Uncle would take several deep breaths, inhaling the rich spring smell of the earth. He proudly pointed out to Hua Fan how the Chinese method of gardening was superior to the *lo fon*'s. The soil was piled up into raised rectangular beds. The seeds were then scattered, covering the entire area. In contrast, the *lo fons* planted in long rows separated by paths. A wasteful use of space. Elder Uncle had saved the seeds from last year's plants. There were beds of *bak choy, toy tchlem,* mustard greens, and snow peas. The snow peas climbed up a framework of twigs along the west side of the garden.

"Look Hua Fan, look." Elder Uncle was inspecting a winter melon plant. Hua Fan walked carefully between the beds and bent down. He gently lifted the young dusky-green leaves and saw a tiny green flower bud attached to the vine. Hua Fan looked at his uncle and smiled.

"We'll have to take good care of this, eh, Hua Fan. Make sure it's covered when the nights get cold."

"Yes, Elder Uncle, yes."

Elder Uncle moved to a second winter melon plant. He tenderly parted the leaves, like a loving parent loosening the grip of a baby. There was another tiny green bud. Beaming with satisfaction, he looked at Hua Fan. "If we take special care with these plants, we can look forward to winter melon soup even in December." Hua Fan nodded silently, stood up and quickly turned to go inside.

That evening as they were finishing their evening meal, Elder Uncle said to Hua Fan. "You have become like a son to me. You are not a big man, but you are hard-working and honest. You know how to endure life in *Gam Sun*, how to eat bitter. When I die this business will be yours."

"Elder Uncle, I owe you a great deal, but you mustn't

talk about such matters. You still have lots of time."

Elder Uncle had been here so long that he rarely talked about going back. His wife was getting old, beyond child bearing. His two daughters were married, now the responsibility of other men. There was nothing more for him to do but work and send money home. But not Hua Fan. He would not stay in the Gold Mountain. He would return home. He would be rich enough to marry the prettiest girl in the village, be respected by everyone who lived there. He wanted to know that if he claimed "number two richest man in the village" no one would claim number one.

"But Hua Fan, I'm getting old. This business is all I have. Now, tell me what news is there in the letter from China."

"Not much," responded Hua Fan and right away he knew that *Gam Sun* and Elder Uncle would be harder to leave than he had ever dreamed.

The next Sunday, Hua Fan and Elder Uncle walked to a stream at the edge of town. They each carried a round bamboo basket and a knife. When they came to the edge of the stream, they stopped. The clear water sparkled, flowing over a riverbed of rocks and mud. Along the banks and into the middle of the stream grew thick beds of water cress, like clumps of dark green curly hair. Hua Fan sat down on a large rock, took a deep breath of late spring air, and looked up at the cloudless blue sky. Silhouetted against the blue were dark tree branches, sprouting tender green leaves. Elder Uncle already had his shoes and socks off and was rolling up the legs of his trousers.

"Hua Fan don't sit and do nothing. Start moving. There's lots of work back in the laundry. You're wasting time."

"All right, all right," said Hua Fan good-naturedly, and he started to remove his shoes and socks as he watched Elder Uncle wade gingerly into the stream.

Elder Uncle gasped, "Eiiiyah!"

"Is it cold?" called Hua Fan.

"Freezing," shuddered Elder Uncle.

Hua Fan slowly stepped into the stream of clear fast moving water, feeling all at once the hard rocks and the soft sinking mud. Both men bent over to grasp bunches of the dark green plants with one hand and slice the bases of the stalks with the other.

Hua Fan was thinking about the taste of water cress soup, the first bowl of the season, when suddenly he felt a shower of stones pelting him on the back. He and Elder Uncle looked up and saw a group of boys standing above on the riverbank. They were laughing as they threw their stones. "Look! The chinks eat grass!" Hua Fan ran up the slope with his knife still in his hand, the blade glinting in the sun. The boys turned and ran.

Elder Uncle called out, "Hua Fan, stop. Don't be foolish. What chance have you got?" He walked toward Hua Fan and handed him his basket of water cress, his shoes and socks. Hua Fan took everything and stomped on ahead, cursing under his breath. Elder Uncle sighed and followed behind.

That night Elder Uncle simmered the water cress in a stock of pork bones. Hua Fan savoured the flavour of the soup in his mouth. It was rich and tangy with a slight clear bitter edge. But it was not enough to erase the smouldering anger that he still felt toward the white devil boys. He couldn't understand how Elder Uncle never seemed to let it affect him. It was as if he had wrapped himself in some kind of impenetrable shell that no *lo fon* would ever be able to pierce.

"Hua Fan, stop thinking about those devil boys. Remember, this is not our home. One day we will leave and go back to China." This was the opening Hua Fan had been waiting for. "Elder Uncle, my mother is ill. The village schoolteacher wrote and told me." But before he could continue, Elder Uncle interrupted.

"Yes, Hua Fan, I know. I am going back. I must go home to China." He put down his rice bowl and chopsticks and looked steadily at Hua Fan. "As head of the family, I must return to China. My own wife is getting old. Your mother, my dead brother's wife is ill. And I, too, am old."

Hua Fan stopped eating and stared at his uncle. "But it's my mother who is sick. I must see her before she dies."

"Hua Fan, she may recover. Anyway, when I return I will tell her all about you, how you've been like a son to me, how hard you have worked. And if it is meant to be, I will see that she dies in peace."

"But Elder Uncle, how will I manage without you? I couldn't manage all by myself."

"You'll be fine. What is there to know about washing clothes? I will find someone in the village to come and join you. You will not be alone for too long."

"Elder Uncle..."

"You are still young. One day you will return and take a wife. Don't you see *Gam Sun* is our only chance for a better life? For the future generation? I have been a luckless man. My life has been nothing but hard work. Maybe yours will be different, who knows? But if you work hard, for certain your children will have something better."

Hua Fan couldn't believe his ears. He wanted to scream, *No! I have no intention of staying! Don't you understand how much I hate it here. I'm not like you. I don't want to be like you! I need to go home.* But he felt as if his vocal chords had been slashed, dangling uselessly inside his throat. All along he had assumed that he would be the one to return. It had never occurred to him that Elder Uncle might also want to go back. The old man seemed so adjusted to life in *Gam Sun*, to being an outsider.

Elder Uncle pleaded, "Don't you see? If I don't go back now, it might be too late?"

Hua Fan's lips felt dry as he opened his mouth and swallowed another spoonful of soup. He looked at the rows of wooden troughs along one wall, the stacks of bamboo baskets in a corner. In the middle of the wooden floor stood the washing machine, a looming silent water buffalo, a sentry standing on guard, preventing escape. As he looked again at Elder Uncle, Hua Fan saw no hint of triumph. Instead he saw a bottomless depth of sadness. For the first time he saw the heavy lines in the old man's face, the mouth set in a line of grim resignation, the sagging corners of the eyes with a tiny flicker of hope. His heart wrenched; surrendering, he understood Elder Uncle's loneliness in this land of strangers, his silent dream of returning home to rest, to die.

"Yes, Elder Uncle," Hua Fan swallowed. "I see."

4

COLD FOOD

According to May-Yen Lum, all the illnesses of the Western world could be traced to the consumption of cold food. But whenever she said to her daughter, "You shouldn't eat so much cold food. You know, ice cream, potato salad. Very bad. Very hard to digest. Sit in the bottom of your stomach. Turn to mould, "Su looked at her and smiled dismissively. Even when May-Yen shouted after her, "Oh, I know, just because you're young and strong now. You can fight those bad effects. You just wait until you're older. Then you'll know." Su still didn't really listen.

May-Yen was sitting in the living room of the apartment that she shared with her stepson, Kenny Lum, and his family. It was above his restaurant, the Lucky Star. Her daughter, Su, was sitting across from her on a gold vinyl stool, their knees just touching. Su spoke slowly with careful concern as she leaned toward her mother and stroked her hand, feeling the swollen, arthritic joints. The conversation had already been repeated several times. "Mah, try not to worry too much about the cancer in your breast. The doctor said it hasn't spread. He can cut it out and that will probably be it." Secretly, Su was hoping, "If I can just move her along, with any luck I'll get home with enough time to finish Jason's psychological assessment." Jason, the frustratingly bright kid who was in grade four and could barely read.

May-Yen looked at her daughter. The soothing tone of her voice, her eyes overflowing with understanding when she didn't really understand was so frustrating. May-Yen knew that she should be grateful that her daughter spoke English so well and was so willing to look after her needs at the hospital. But she just couldn't help being annoyed with Su who was so confident of the *lo fon* doctors, with her daughter who had such faith in *lo fon* medicine. "It's not cancer, you know. The doctors here don't know."

"What are you saying?"

"I know what's really wrong. My body is mouldy inside. It's from eating all that *lo fon* food, that Canadian food especially the cold stuff, you know, ice cream, cold meat, potato salad...."

"Mah, I really think you should listen to the doctor. He knows...."

"Dock-tah! Dock-tah! What does he know? I know. I haven't been careful enough. And now I'm all mouldy inside."

Su took a deep breath and patted her mother's hand again. She was working hard to suppress a smile as she imagined her mother's stomach all woolly with minute blue and grey fungi. "Mah, just try and relax. Try not to worry too much. Let me take care of everything." May-Yen turned her head away from her daughter. She clenched her lips tightly, not allowing a word, a sound, to escape.

Su got up and returned to the packing. She vacuumed up the dust and finished stacking the cardboard boxes, old vinyl suitcases and green garbage bags into a cohesive pile, while May-Yen sat forlornly on a green chesterfield watching her daughter's every movement, wringing her hands like a set of giant worry beads.

May-Yen remembered thinking that cancer was a Western disease, but now Chinese people were getting it. The people who had been careless about eating all that *lo fon* food. Didn't they know any better? We Chinese are raised on rice — rice that's hot and soft and cushions the inside of your stomach, radiating a gentle source of heat. But the ice cream, the potato salad — so cold and heavy. You could tell by the way that it coated the inside of your mouth with a thick film that it was bad for you. Food should be clear and savoury and leave your mouth feeling cleansed but your stomach full and warm.

But now the doctors were saying that she had cancer. Three days earlier, May-Yen had been on the phone to tell her daughter what her doctor had told her — or at least what Kenny had told her the doctor had said. When May-Yen finished, Su insisted on speaking to Kenny. Between them they decided that May-Yen should go and stay with Su in Toronto. Of course it made sense. Kenny wouldn't have time for all those doctor's visits. He and his wife ran the Lucky Star by themselves without hired help. It wasn't that May-Yen wasn't grateful to her children, especially to her daughter, who spoke English so well and who had a university education. She just couldn't help thinking, I wasn't even asked.

Su finished the packing, checked her watch, and went downstairs to the restaurant. She was anxious to leave her brother's apartment. She found the low ceilings and lack of light depressing and oppressive. Her mother's bedroom looked out at a brick wall only three feet away. Su returned with her husband, Harry, and their two young sons. The boys rushed to give their grandmother a hug. May-Yen absent-mindedly patted them on their shoulders while she watched her daughter and her son-in-law dismantle her fortress of worldly possessions, carrying everything down a long flight of wooden stairs.

Su's fingers tapped out a quiet rhythm as she held the car door open for her mother. May-Yen slowly brought her legs around the back seat, and with her daughter's help, edged her feet on to the sidewalk. She held Su's arm and carefully walked up the path to the large red brick house. May-Yen was surprised to see yellow and red leaves scattered all over the lawn. There were no trees around the restaurant and she rarely stepped outside. Harry and her grandsons walked quickly past several times, each time carrying another package.

Su had cleared out a room next to the bathroom in anticipation of her mother's arrival. May-Yen, exhausted from climbing the stairs, sat slumped in a chair. Su looked around in disbelief at her mother's belongings — a careless collection of cardboard boxes, suitcases and bulging green garbage bags. A mingling of smells from her childhood, of camphor, spearmint and mothballs was beginning to permeate the room.

May-Yen watched her daughter walk over to a stack of boxes and lift the lid off the top one. Inside, carefully folded, was a pink chiffon gown with a full skirt of many layers. Su took the dress out, shook it, and held it in front of her with arms extended, and looked at her mother in disbelief. "Mah, why are you keeping this? This thing is twenty years old. I wore it when I was the bridesmaid at Kenny's wedding."

May-Yen sat up straight. "*Eiyah!* That dress cost a lot of money. So what if I keep it?"

"But Mah, it's never going to be in style again. Don't you think this is a bit ridiculous?" Su opened another box and found a pair of sheepskin boots that she had bought for her mother many Christmases ago — never worn, still in the original package. She knew better than to say anything more. She knew that her mother was watching her, that her mother saved everything. And anything that was new stayed new — for those elusive "good" occasions.

In another box there were jars filled with water chestnut powder for diarrhoea, gnarled brown roots for tonic soups, square green envelopes of bitter tea for influenza, and vials of pink *Po Chai* pills for nausea — talismans against the effects of Western food. She sighed as she looked at her mother's possessions, which now filled the room, providing May-Yen with protection and security like an invisible cloak. Her treasures and her demons were stuffed into those boxes. As bitter as May-Yen's memories might be, she was not about to part with them. Su shook her head and left to write Jason's psychological assessment.

More than forty years earlier, Su arrived in Canada with her mother on a propeller-driven airplane. They were met at the airport by her aunt and uncle, since her father lived several hours from Toronto. The next day she met her father, Lum Mun Lek, for the first time. He nodded at May-Yen and patted their daughter on the head, saying her name, "Su Jing." He was a small wizened man with large calloused hands and lines of suffering deeply engraved into his face.

Later that afternoon, Su and May-Yen followed Mun Lek aboard a Gray Coach bus that took them to his hand laundry in Sydney, a small town in Ontario. Su sat with her mother while her father sat across the aisle. Throughout the journey, her mother suffered from motion sickness. When she wasn't vomiting into a brown paper bag, she sat with a look of desperation, squeezing Su's hand until the knuckle joints popped against each other. Her father sat with the muscles in his face taut, his eyes bewildered, staring straight ahead, saying almost nothing.

After a four-hour ride, they arrived in Sydney. Mun Lek warned them about the snow and ice on the sidewalks. When May-Yen stepped off the bus, she slipped. The bus driver grabbed her by the arm and she awkwardly steadied herself. Mun Lek picked up the large tan leather suitcase and carried it to the laundry. Su and May-Yen struggled behind with the smaller bags.

The laundry was their home. May-Yen looked up and saw a tired building, the paint flaking and blistered on the wooden exterior like boils on a bad complexion. From the front door she could see the railway tracks. She stepped inside after her husband and saw a long, dim, silent place filled with ancient machinery — a large wooden-barrel washing machine with a motor attached, wooden laundry tubs for rinsing, and an old table tightly wrapped with years of worn sheets and blankets. In the middle of the table stood an upright iron, cold and still in an expanse of white. There was a slight depression in the floor in front of the table where Mun Lek always stood while ironing. It was late afternoon and the narrow shadows cast by the equipment stretched long and thin across the floorboards like the bars of a prison. To the side was a small room with a double bed. Su would sleep in the middle, her parents lying rigid on either side of her.

After the Second World War, Mun Lek had returned to China from Canada to look for a wife, someone to help in the laundry. His prospects were not good. He was over fifty, a widower with a family of two grown sons; he was considered past the prime of his life. He ran a hand laundry. Everyone knew that the restaurant business offered a more promising future. When May-Yen met Mun Lek, she was over thirty, also considered past her prime. She had lost her husband during the war and was living with her brother-in-law, who considered her another mouth to feed. The meagre earnings she brought home from her job as a clerk in a government office were received with contempt. A marriage between May-Yen and Mun Lek provided the perfect solution for both.

Just before Su's birth in Hong Kong, her father had returned to Canada. In the small town of Sydney, he'd opened another hand laundry where he worked alone. There were two Chinese establishments in the town; the hand laundry and a restaurant. May-Yen was the first Chinese woman in the town, and Su was the first Chinese child.

Work in the laundry started the day after their arrival. For the next fifteen years until Mun Lek's death, May Yen worked by his side. Su watched her mother sort clothing, mend collars and cuffs, replace buttons, darn socks — the belongings of strangers, their acrid body odours lingering on their clothes. At times May-Yen wondered out loud, "My God! Same watery eyes, same big noses. *All-ah* same to me!"

On wash days, May-Yen helped her husband tame the wooden barrel machine that agitated the clothes until they were clean. She pulled clothes out of wooden tubs of icy rinse water and cranked them by hand through wringers. In the summer, the clothes were hung outside on lines to dry. Her single vanity had been her finely pored, pale, ivory skin. Each summer she watched in silent surrender as her skin turned brown and the faint lines on her face grew deeper and deeper.

Every evening after supper, she fed sheets, tea towels and tablecloths through ironing rollers, transforming limp, wrinkled bits of cloth into yards of smooth, sleek fabric that looked like full-blown sails on a ship. She also produced three meals a day. Lunch and supper were unthinkable without hot homemade soup. Her husband rarely spoke, except to give orders. Their meals were eaten in silence.

May-Yen resigned herself to her new life. But sometimes she looked at her daughter, her eyes pools of unfathomable sadness. "There was a time, back in China, when I used to go to movies, maybe play *mah jong* in the evenings. There was a time when I had friends."

Fifteen years later, when her husband died, May-Yen moved in with Mun Lek's son, Kenny and his family. After Mun Lek's funeral, Su stayed at the laundry with her mother for a week. She helped her mother pack her belongings into the tan leather suitcase that May-Yen had brought from Hong Kong and into an assortment of brown cardboard boxes. At the end of the week Kenny drove down from Urquhart in his blue station-wagon. Su caught a Toronto bus back to university.

There was no choice for May-Yen, but to move in with Kenny and his family, into a small bedroom in the apartment above the Lucky Star. From the beginning, her bedroom was stacked to the ceiling with boxes full of ancient belongings. The bed was pushed, flush to the wall and more boxes were crammed underneath.

When May-Yen walked through the wooden swinging door into the restaurant kitchen after her first night in her new home, her stepson pointed at a bushel of unpeeled potatoes. Everyday there were baskets of carrots, celery and onions waiting to be peeled, washed and chopped. Everyday there were stacks of plates that needed scraping and pots that need scrubbing.

Two days after bringing her mother to Toronto, Su sat next to her in the oncologist's waiting room at Toronto General Hospital. The receptionist had a look of impatience and amusement as she watched May-Yen fumble with her gnarled, arthritic fingers, trying to remove her hospital card from a clear plastic bag containing several identity cards, with each card again individually wrapped in another clear plastic bag and bundled with an elastic. She refused all help. Su remembered once suggesting to her mother that she buy a wallet with slots for her cards. May-Yen had indignantly responded, "What do I need a wallet for? You should be like me and sew pockets inside your jackets and pants. That way nobody can rob you. And you save money. See, no need for expensive wallets and purses!"

Su sighed. She couldn't help thinking that although her mother had never been victimized by a pickpocket, a simple purchase required her to nearly undress in public.

After a short wait, Su led her mother into the brightly lit examination room. She helped May-Yen remove her multiple layers of clothing — a jacket, two sweaters, a blouse and an undershirt. Then a young doctor entered the room. As Su translated the instructions, "Turn this way. Turn that way. Lift your arm." May-Yen curled her lips inward in that special way of hers. Not once did her eyes leave the floor.

When they were finished, Su led her mother to the elevator. They went up several levels then down a long corridor. Su walked slowly while May-Yen worked hard to keep up. Her eyes, like those of a frightened bird, darted from side to side, trying to make sense of the different offices and waiting rooms.

They were taken into a sterile examination room by a gentle female technician. The giant mammogram machine, with its menacing, pivoting arm loomed in front of May-Yen who stood naked from the waist up. Under the fluorescent light her skin looked thin and parched with finely etched wrinkles like the scales of a fish. Her shoulders were hunched; her breasts hung empty. She stood shivering. Su carefully translated the instructions: "Face this wall. Place your breast flat on the shelf. Now place it vertically. Now face the other wall."

A month later, May-Yen was propped up with pillows in her hospital bed. Leaning forward, she noisily slurped down a clear chicken broth. Su was sitting relaxed on a chair.

Watching her mother, she realized how surprised she had been by the routine quality of the operation.

A nurse poked her head in the door, "Your mother's amazing. Considering she's eighty, she's come through the anaesthetic really well. And her incision is healing, well, beautifully!" Su translated for her mother, nodding in agreement with the nurse.

May-Yen said to Su, "You tell the nurse the real reason I'm recovering so well is because all my life I make sure I eat hot food and drink lots of Chinese tonics." The nurse, not understanding a word, stood smiling in anticipation.

Finally Su said, turning to the nurse, "My mother wants to thank you for the excellent care." After the nurse left, Su smiled to herself, remembering how Kenny had once compared May-Yen to an old door that still opened and closed, but the hinges were getting rustier and squeakier.

The next day, when Su returned to the hospital, May-Yen was talking to a new roommate. May-Yen motioned eagerly with her arm. "Su, come meet Wong Mo. She's the same age as me and she has an apartment in a seniors' building." Wong Mo was in the hospital for minor surgery. She was a short woman with a body as round as her face. She had high cheek bones and eyes that crinkled into folds when she laughed.

"Ah, so you're the daughter," said Wong Mo. "You know how to talk to the doctors and you have a university degree. Very smart."

"Oh, not that smart. Just lucky that I came to Canada so young," Su responded, trying hard to keep that edge of annoyance from her voice. She hated it when her mother bragged about her. No matter how hard she tried, she was unable to convince her mother that although she, Su, was the only one in her family to have a degree, it really was no big deal to anyone else. But this time May-Yen hadn't even noticed her daughter's irritation. She was too busy talking to her new friend. And when Su left her mother that afternoon, she felt for the first time, free of guilt.

It turned out that May-Yen and Wong Mo were born in neighbouring villages. But when they discovered that their husbands had died in the same year, they knew they were destined to be friends.

When May-Yen left the hospital, she returned to her daughter's home. Though it was unspoken, she knew that she would not return to her stepson's apartment above the Lucky Star.

It had been two years to the day since May-Yen's operation. She was lying awake in bed, in her daughter's home, listening to taps run, toilets flush and doors bang. A few minutes later, she heard the heavy front door shut for the last time. Everyone was gone. Finally! The house was now empty except for her. It was safe to get up. Yesterday she had desperately needed to void while Su, Harry and the two boys were preparing for work and school. As hard as she tried to be fast on the toilet, she knew she was taking what seemed an eternity. Although nothing was said, Su's impatience filled the air like a bad smell. It was during times like this that May-Yen found herself thinking: Maybe I should fall. What if I fell while they were rushing around? What then?

The last two years spent living with Su and her family had not been all that bad. She spent a good part of each day sleeping; but she also talked for at least an hour every day to Wong *Mo*. Thank God for Wong *Mo!* May-Yen had visited her several times in her seniors' apartment. Twice, she had stayed for several days. On her last visit, Wong *Mo* told her that a larger unit was being vacated. Perhaps she and May-Yen could share it. As Wong *Mo* spoke, May-Yen took an extra breath and felt a slight ruffling in her chest, a long forgotten yearning. She realized that deep inside she was like a piece of dry earth, parched and cracked. Ever since she had first set foot in this country, her *thlem, gwon*, her heart and liver, had been suspended. Might they finally settle? She felt the question echoing inside her belly, "A home of my own?" She shuddered with fear as she realized that this would be her last and only chance.

May-Yen slowly pushed herself up on the mattress and inched her legs around so that they dangled over the side of the bed. This first rising after a night's sleep was always the most difficult. Her bones were like creased pieces of ancient paper. They had to be unfolded oh, so carefully. Any sudden movement or overexertion and her bones, like yellowed paper, would crumble. When May-Yen entered the kitchen, the crystal vase of red tulips caught her eye. She frowned and muttered under her breath at her daughter's extravagance — spending money on something that you couldn't eat or wear, that lasted such a short while before being thrown out. Then she saw the small familiar stainless steel pot on the stove. Su had left the porridge on low heat for her. She half-filled a cup with water and added it to the pot and stirred. Her daughter cooked porridge like the *lo fons* — thick and lumpy. May-Yen liked it smooth and runny. Some days she added an egg for nutrition and texture.

The food at Su's was not so bad. May-Yen liked spaghetti with meat sauce; the barbecued chicken was nicely flavoured; and Harry always produced a well-cooked roast on Sundays. But May-Yen remained unconvinced that pizza in a box was a fit meal for anyone. She thought of all the little things that she missed like winter melon soup, dried salted fish and fermented bean curd. Her mouth watering, she felt petty and ungrateful.

No one ever told her, but May-Yen knew. She knew the real reason why she never returned to Kenny's. When she came out of the hospital, he had emphasized several times how much better off she'd be to stay at Su's. He had seized her cancer as an opportunity to toss her out, like a worn-out slipper. She had outlived her use at the restaurant. For the last few years, she had been more a hindrance than a help, an obstacle underfoot while Kenny was rushing around the kitchen. Yet in a perverse way she missed the restaurant. Looking around her daughter's kitchen with every item in its place, and the Formica counters freshly wiped, she again acknowledged to herself that things were quite bearable. She told herself that she should be grateful to have a daughter who took her in, slotting her into a busy schedule without missing a beat. Su did everything. She washed the clothes, cooked the meals, did the dishes, kept a spotless house, managed everyone's comings and goings. Her energy and efficiency were truly formidable; she was like a general coolly leading her army. Even when May-Yen tried to help, Su told her to sit down. In her daughter's house she was like a perpetual guest. At Kenny's, even though she was resented, she had a role. As long as she was able, she was an extra pair of hands, providing free labour.

May-Yen looked around again at the gleaming counters and the vase of red tulips. She thought about Wong *Mo*, about sharing a home with her friend. Tonight she would tell Su that she was moving out, that finally she was taking flight. And she chuckled to herself, as she imagined the look on her daughter's face.

Three months later, Su visited her mother in the new apartment that she shared with Wong *Mo*. Two months earlier she and her half-brother had moved May-Yen and her boxes into her apartment. Su and Kenny gave her a selection of old furniture. At first Su had suggested buying some new items, but May-Yen would have none of it — an unnecessary waste of money. Kenny gave her an old brown plaid chesterfield. Wong *Mo* already had a used red arborite kitchen table. Su gave them her second television and bought them a large electric wall clock for the kitchen. The walls in the bedroom, the kitchen and the living room were decorated with Chinese movie star calendars.

Su sat at the kitchen table sipping tea as her mother brought her a plate of steamed dumplings. Wong *Mo* followed behind, carrying a bowl filled with a hot, brown pungent brew.

"Su, your mother made this, just for you," said Wong *Mo*.

"After you told me you were coming, I decided to make this soup. I got up early. It's been simmering all day. Very good for women — made from deer antlers — keeps your womb and your organs warm," added May-Yen eagerly.

"Mah, I'm not going to have room for dinner tonight," protested Su, looking at the food on the kitchen table.

"Well, just eat a few dumplings, but drink all the soup,"

said May-Yen. "I've got more for you to take home." Wong Mo nodded in agreement.

Su picked up the white ceramic spoon and gently slurped the brown liquid. The two older women looked on approvingly.

"Now remember, the soup is just for women. No good for men," added Wong Mo.

"Just eat a few dumplings. Your favourite — shrimp and chicken," insisted May-Yen. "Too much for us."

No kidding, thought Su to herself. You old girls have made enough to feed an army. She grinned at her mother and Wong Mo as she put down her spoon and picked up a dumpling with her chopsticks.

Watching her mother and Wong Mo fuss in the kitchen, Su thought about the woman who hid and worked all those years in the shadows of her father's laundry. And again in the kitchen of her brother's restaurant. Was she finally seeing a glimmer of the woman who had lived and worked in China so long ago? Su felt a flush of heat in her cheeks as she remembered her protests when May-Yen told her about moving. Why do you want to move? I do everything here for you. You don't have to do a thing. You're going to have a hard time managing.

An hour later, Su stood at the apartment door, ready to leave. First she hugged Wong Mo, then her mother. May-Yen gave her daughter two white plastic bags of food. Su walked down the apartment hallway with a bag of dumplings dangling over her wrist and both hands around a jar of hot tonic soup wrapped inside a plastic bag. Taking special care to keep the jar upright, she held it against herself, feeling its heat warming her hands and her chest.

5

THE LUCKY WEDDING

IT WAS SUNDAY MORNING, THE DAY AFTER VALENTINE'S DAY. Sandra had been married to Victor for eleven days and no one in her family knew. She was driving to her brother's restaurant for her mother's birthday celebration. Fortunately the traffic was light. It was hard to concentrate on the road and at the same time, carry on an imaginary conversation with family members. Even when alone, Sandra was always careful to rehearse in her mind what she would say. Lurking just around the corner was madness. After all if you started talking out loud to imaginary people, you might never stop. In fact, the arguing inside her head had been incessant for the last week. Her mother was lodged in her head like a permanent resident, an unwanted guest who wasn't budging. When she woke up in the morning, she saw her mother's disapproving broad face, floating above her like a rain cloud. Her first thought was, "How will I break the news to her?" Even last night while Victor was on top of her, thoughts of her mother edged slyly, surreptitiously into her consciousness. Her mother was uncontrollable, coming unbidden into her mind like a wild wind brushing everything else aside. A week ago, Sandra had vowed to herself that during lovemaking she would only sigh or moan. Talking was strictly prohibited. Victor would never understand her crying out Mah during a moment of ecstasy.

As Sandra left the apartment on Howland Avenue after having lunch with Victor, he had asked her again, "Are you sure you don't want me to come with you?" But Sandra had been resolute. She knew her family, that is, she knew her mother. And this would be the best way. Of course she could handle it.

Sandra had decided on the direct approach. She would simply march briskly into her brother's restaurant with her chin held high. But not too high. She didn't want to appear cocky. Then she would open her arms wide and declare, "Hey, guess what everybody!" Earlier that morning she had practised her smile in front of the mirror. A wide, natural smile, not so wide, though, that it appeared forced. But as she drove off the main highway and on to the two-lane road leading to Urquhart, she began to have even more doubts. The confidence that had been so solid and secure early in the morning was melting, vaporizing, leaving a distinct hollow in her heart.

Perhaps her plan was just a little too bold, too brash. Better to simply make a quiet, friendly entrance, then find a private moment with her mother. Tell her first. Would that be the best way? The problem, though, was that there was no best way. Running off and getting married without informing your family was bad enough. But Sandra had run off and married Victor. And Victor was a *lo fon*. Not that being a *lo fon*, a white foreigner, was entirely hopeless. You just weren't supposed to marry one. To make matters worse, Victor's livelihood was suspiciously unreliable. He was an artist, a painter, someone who worked with his hands, like a labourer.

Sandra knew that her mother was still hoping that one day Sandra would bring home a nice, educated Chinese boy, a lawyer or an accountant. She also reminded Sandra that 1988 was an especially auspicious year. If they planned things carefully, she could be married in August, the eighth month. But now that Sandra was twenty-nine, things were becoming desperate. Any moment now, she might turn into an old maid, a desiccated little old lady. Recently, whenever Mrs Low spoke to her daughter, her voice took on a tone of controlled hysteria. When they spoke on the phone together, she always managed to squeeze in, "Sanda-*ah*, tomorrow you're going to turn into a *lob nui*, an old girl. Vah... nobody *boo nay*, nobody take you." To Sandra those words, *boo nay*, felt more like "snatch" than "take." She supposed that after a certain point, she wouldn't even be snatchable.

Mrs Low even went to the trouble of giving her daughter's graduation picture to Mrs Yee, the well-known matchmaker in Toronto. She knew that by *Gam Sun* standards, Sandra would be considered fairly desirable and the matchmaker would collect a handsome fee from the family of the prospective husband. After all, Sandra had a university education and a job with a decent salary and was not bad-looking. And there were no moles in unlucky positions on Sandra's face, and — as far as she knew — none on her body. Mrs Low remembered how Betty Kwan had made her daughter have a mole removed from underneath the inside corner of her left eye. The mole stood in the path of tears: a symbol of the family wealth being washed away. No family would willingly embrace a bride whose face bore such an obvious omen of poverty.

During her last visit to the restaurant, Sandra's mother took her aside and showed her pictures of three different young men who were looking for wives. One was an accountant and two were computer experts. Sandra smiled uncomfortably and said, "I'm not ready to get married yet."

"Not ready!" said Mrs Low in exasperation. "You're twenty-nine. Soon it's going to be too late." Sandra merely smiled and shrugged her shoulders. "By the time you're ready, you'll be too old."

Sandra fiddled with the silver bangles on her wrist, and flicked her hair over her shoulder. "Mah, they just don't look like my type."

"But all nice boys. No pocked skin or bad teeth. All good jobs, don't smoke and drive their own cars."

"I don't know. They're just not my type."

"The boys you like — all seem so *goo gai*, strange, weird. *Lo fons*, okay, sometimes. The one who liked you in high school, now he was nice, the rich boy, the one whose father was a doctor."

"Mah, that was a long time ago."

"But the ones now, the one with the long hair and no real job."

"Ma-ah." That was the signal to end — that special inflection in Sandra's tone. They both knew the unspoken reason for Sandra's resistance was Victor.

When Sandra was in university, several of her professors made passes at her. One of them was quite persistent. He was a hobby photographer and wanted her to model for him. At first it seemed innocent enough. But one day when she arrived at his studio, he looked at her with his rheumy grey eyes just a second too long. He was holding a red silk garment in his hands, absent-mindedly stroking it with long thin fingers. Without saying a word, he passed the dress to her. It was a silk cheongsam with deep side slits meant to expose the thighs. Sandra took one look and left. The professor's interest in her had always seemed sexual and protective at the same time. But now she couldn't help wondering if he just wanted to live out a fantasy of making love to Susie Wong. Victor, though, was different.

Sandra and Victor had met a few years before at the University of Toronto. She was a librarian in the main library. Victor was an artist, a painter. Sandra still remembered the day he came into the library gallery to look at an exhibit of paintings. She remembered the loose plaid shirt and the paint-splattered denim jeans. His shoulder-length hair was clean, freshly washed. Sandra was immediately suspicious as she watched him examine the pictures. He seemed far too interested in the way each frame was mounted on the wall. Victor had been aware of Sandra right from the beginning, of her unwavering stare drilling into his back. Afterward, he walked directly to her desk. "Those paintings are mine you know. I painted them."

Sandra leaned slightly back in her chair as Victor stood with his arms propped on her desk, his body angled in her direction. She smelled just a faint trace of aftershave. He had read her unspoken suspicions so accurately that she found herself at a loss for words. Once again she was glad of her dark complexion, hiding her blush of embarrassment. Victor straightened up and started to laugh. Sandra looked up and noticed that his teeth were straight, white and perfectly shaped. Then in a complete change of tone, he asked her out for coffee. Sandra smiled and said "Yes."

When Victor asked Sandra to marry him, she was only somewhat surprised. After all, they had been living together for over a year. Between them, they had developed a mutual routine of quiet compatibility.

They lived in an apartment on the second floor of a large house on Howland Avenue. Their furnishings were few, but carefully chosen — a small grey sofa, an olive green armchair, a second-hand oriental carpet, a stereo set, a torchère lamp and a bookcase made of wooden planks and bricks. Victor's large canvasses of conflicting, writhing colours decorated the plain white walls. And together they lavished their attention on the *ficus benjamina* that thrived in a sunny corner of their bay window.

Sandra remembered exactly when Victor proposed. It was memorable for the ordinariness of the timing. They had been clearing away the dishes together after eating their order-in pizza. The words just popped out of Victor's mouth. "I think we should get married." Sandra was surprised at how quickly she said yes. If she didn't say it fast enough, he might not ask her again. It was only then that she realized how important it was to her that their union be official. For over a year she had ignored her own feelings and desires, allowing them to breathe only between the layers of her skin.

When they first met, Sandra had taken Victor to several family functions, but then he gradually stopped going. Sandra's family was never overtly unfriendly. But there was something unnerving about the way Mrs Low looked at Victor when she greeted him and the way she spoke about him in Chinese to whomever happened to be around. He picked out his name in the jumble of Chinese sounds. The unflattering tone of her voice made him feel just slightly uncomfortable. Often he felt ignored and Sandra's fussing made it worse. He got the distinct feeling that although his presence was never actively discouraged, neither was it enthusiastically welcomed.

So when Victor stopped showing up, Sandra's family carried on as if he no longer existed. He was Sandra's secret and one that they didn't particularly want to share. For several years Sandra went along with this charade. But when she and Victor got married at City Hall with her best friend, Gail, for a witness, Sandra wanted to tell them, but didn't know how. She was sick of these family pretenses. She wanted out.

Sandra parked her car outside her brother's restaurant, the Golden Gate. More than ten years ago, Glen and their father had purchased the restaurant from Bill Woo. Shortly after taking over, their father died of a sudden heart attack.

Sandra reached into the back seat and grabbed a bag filled with a barbecued duck and a strip of roast pork and a second bag filled with oranges. After getting out of the car, she took a deep breath and opened the door to the restaurant.

Everyone was laughing and talking, clustered around a table at the back of the dining room. Just behind them was a room divider decorated with a golden dragon and a phoenix. At one time it must have been striking, providing a focus for the room. But it now looked tired and shabby. Dustballs were lodged in the scales of the dragon and a layer of dust dulled the tail feathers of the phoenix. Christmas decorations were still dangling between the lights. Bill Woo had sold her

brother a thriving business, but Glen had taken it for granted, and Sandra knew without even asking that business was
poor.

Her older sister, "movie star" Marilyn, was the first one
to notice her arrival. The three of them had been named
after Hollywood celebrities: Glen, after Glen Ford; Marilyn,
after Marilyn Monroe; and Sandra after Sandra Dee. But
Marilyn was the only one to really live up to her namesake.
Her voice was a husky, velvet purr, and her movements were
studied and seductive, like a sex kitten.

"Here she is, the *hoo sung*, our Canadian-born," Marilyn
called out to everyone. "Sandra, you're here at last. We've
been waiting for ages."

"Oh, the traffic was really heavy."

Marilyn's left eyebrow went up and she looked at her
husband, Walter. Everyone knew Sandra was lying.

Sandra leaned over and gave her mother a hug. "Happy
birthday, Mah."

Then she walked into the kitchen. Glen was standing at
the counter, his head down, slicing vegetables. His wife,
May, was in front of the sink, washing a large pot of rice.
Sandra handed Glen the bag of barbecued meats.

He looked up from his chopping. "Oh! Hi. Thanks, how
much do I owe you?"

"No, no. It's okay." Sandra waved her hand and shook
her head in protest.

"No, no, I should pay," said Glen, facing down, still
chopping.

"No. It's *okay*," Sandra insisted emphatically. As Glen
started to reach for his wallet, Sandra walked into the dining
room, muttering to herself. She hated these charades, always

having to be alert, knowing when *yes* meant *no* and *no* meant *yes*. She glanced back and caught May's twinkling eyes, a knowing smile on her face.

When Sandra returned to the dining room and looked at Marilyn and Walter and their three children and then at her mother, the vestiges of resolve evaporated, leaving her feeling short of breath and dry in the mouth. She helped to set the tables, then sat down to dinner with her family. The food was tasty, or so everyone said. The conversation was incessant, but the only voice Sandra heard was her own, echoing inside her head — a steady monologue, drowning out all the outside voices. This is crazy. Marriage is supposed to be a celebration. I feel like a sneak with a dirty secret that's going to upset everybody. In the end, she just couldn't snip the wire for the family tightrope act.

Two days later, Sandra was on the phone to her mother. "Mah, I have some news. Victor and I got married."

There was silence, followed by "When?"

"Two weeks ago. I was going to tell you at your birthday party. But I decided I wanted to tell just you first."

"Why are you like this? Sneaking off. Not having any-one from your own family at your wedding. Not giving face." Sandra started to fidget with the telephone cord.

"Mah, it wasn't a big affair. We just had a friend as a witness. We got married at City Hall. We're going to have a reception. And we want everybody to come."

"What kind of reception? Chinese or *lo fon*, Canadian?"

"I don't know yet. Victor and I will have to talk about it." She looked at Victor sitting on the sofa, half-heartedly reading the newspaper.

Sandra said goodbye and put down the phone. There was no point in further discussion. She felt like a coward. But her family had never really given Victor a chance. Her mother rarely referred to him by name. She still called him that *gwei loh*, that devil man. The fact that he was an artist didn't help either; his livelihood was suspiciously unreliable. And even worse, as her mother emphasized, he worked with his hands. This was in contrast to Walter, her sister's husband, who was a chartered accountant with a lucrative business, who wore a three-piece suit to work every day, who used his brain to make a living and who served the Chinese community. It was a good thing Victor didn't speak Chinese. Although he intuitively understood her mother's misgivings, at least he never heard the specifics. Her mother would just have to get used to having a white man for a son-in-law.

"Well, how'd your mum take the news?" Victor looked up from the newspaper as Sandra put down the phone and splayed herself out on the armchair.

"She wasn't hysterical. And she didn't disown me."

"That's good. Now what did she say?" Victor asked, carefully folding the paper.

"Oh," Sandra sighed. "The usual guilt trip. What I expected. That my actions slighted the family."

"Did you tell her we'd have a party. Maybe she could help with the planning."

Sandra sat up and shot Victor a look. "Get serious."

Victor and Sandra wanted a very small affair — perhaps a few friends and the immediate family. They were half successful. They invited their few personal friends and the immediate members of Victor's family. But Sandra's mother insisted on inviting distant relatives whom Sandra had not seen since she was a small child.

Sandra obediently took the final guest list and meticulously handwrote each invitation with a fountain pen. The following Sunday she drove to her brother's restaurant to display her efforts to her mother. As she watched the countryside breeze by, she smiled, feeling proud and very pleased with herself.

Mrs Low was sitting at the back of the restaurant. She was reading the Chinese newspaper. Other sections of the paper were scattered on the table. On the wall beside the table was a large Chinese calendar. Each month was adorned by a close-up of a Chinese female movie star. The February calendar girl seemed especially coquettish, her dark eyes flirting with the camera.

Sandra walked briskly into the restaurant. She gave her mother a quick hug, tidied the pile of papers on the table, sat down, and carefully showed her the invitations.

Her mother rested one arm on the table in front of her. The other arm was perched on its elbow, while her hand supported her jaw. She looked at Sandra, then pursed her lips as she shook her head in disapproval. "You can't send invitations like this."

"Why not?" Sandra had spent many hours looking at blank cards before settling on one with a cover that would neither offend nor have a hidden unlucky meaning for the Chinese guests. She purposely avoided anything that was unusual or had a hint of the occult. She finally decided on a woodland scene of a bird gazing thoughtfully at a peaceful blue lake. Who could possibly object to a landscape?

Mrs Low looked at Sandra with complete disbelief.

Surely her daughter couldn't be this ignorant. "You don't know anything. How can you send a card with just one bird? This is a wedding reception. There should at be least two birds."

"But I've written them all out."

"Well send them to the *lo fons* if you want. They don't know any better. But don't send them to the Chinese. They'll think your reception bad luck."

Sandra gathered up the cards and stormed out of the restaurant. She drove off without even noticing her mother running after her. When she reached Howland Avenue, she raced up the stairs to the second floor and unlocked the door. The moment she stepped inside, a feeling of relief rushed over her. Fortunately Victor wasn't home. She needed to be alone. Sandra kicked off her shoes and threw herself lengthwise on the sofa, her head propped up against the arm. She was still trembling and her face was wet with tears. She was livid. But mostly, with herself. Why was she letting her mother affect her like this?

Sandra lay on the sofa with her arm over her eyes, tasting the salty tears that rolled down her cheeks. Everyone in her family understood all those rules of Chinese etiquette and protocol so naturally, so intuitively. Everyone that is, except her. Sandra remembered once having dinner with her family at the home of a wealthy relative. She was eleven. Marilyn was twenty-one and Glen was twenty-four. They were both still living at home. Everyone was seated around a large oval-shaped rosewood table covered with a thick white tablecloth. There was a Lazy Susan in the middle of the table with assorted barbecued meats, stir-fried shrimp with vegetables, a braised stew of beef and dried bean curd. Sandra was very careful not to move the Lazy Susan, to only take from the dishes that were in front of her, and to wait for the adults around the table to initiate the turns. She was also mindful of the way she held her chopsticks, keeping her palm facing up when she reached for food so that her elbow stayed at her side. Marilyn never failed to point out that when Sandra reached for food at the table, she stuck out her elbow, rudely interfering with the space of the person next to her. In her mind she could hear Marilyn admonishing her, "You idiot! Keep your elbow to your side before you jab somebody." Afterwards her mother would shake her head and laugh, "What do you expect from these *hoo sung*, these Canadian-born?" And her father would add, *"Mo Yung*, useless!" and laugh again.

Throughout the entire meal, Sandra had remained very quiet. When the wealthy aunt asked her if she would like more rice, Sandra smiled and immediately replied yes. By the sudden silence in the room, Sandra knew she had committed a major gaffe. But what? Hadn't she simply responded to a question? The wealthy Aunt quickly smiled, took Sandra's rice bowl and returned it to her filled with steaming white rice. Everyone breathed a quiet, but audible sigh of relief.

Afterwards, as they were driving home, her mother explained to her, "When you're having dinner in someone's home and you're asked if you'd like some more, you must always say no."

Sandra looked puzzled, "But why?"

"Don't you know anything?" Marilyn rolled her eyes.

Mrs Low looked exasperated, but continued to explain. "You say no because she might not have enough food."

"Well, if she doesn't have enough, why did she ask in

the first place?"

"Don't you see? If the host doesn't have enough food, she still has to ask in order to save face. But you're supposed to say no, in case there's no food. If there's really enough food then she'll offer again."

"Then can I say yes?"

"No," said Mrs Low emphatically, with a deep sigh. "You still have to say no."

"But why?" asked Sandra, sounding equally exasperated.

"Because when you accept so quickly you sound too eager and greedy."

"You mean I have to be asked three times before I can say yes."

"Don't you see?" Marilyn chimed in. "That way everybody saves face. If the host doesn't have enough food, she's already asked, but you've said no. After she's asked you three times, it means there's lots of food and you don't appear greedy by accepting too quickly."

"These Canadian-born, *hoo sung, Mo Yung,* useless," muttered Mrs Low under her breath.

For the rest of the trip home, Sandra pressed her face against the window, looking out into the darkness, into the headlights of the oncoming cars. Well, if her family wished she were more Chinese, she wished they were more Canadian.

As Sandra rested on her couch in the apartment on Howland Avenue, she realized that things hadn't changed all that much. She still found Chinese etiquette and protocol a quagmire. It was true that once things were explained they made sense. But the problem was that so little came intuitively, the way it came to Marilyn. Everything was in code. It was all so unlike the Canadian way of doing things — forthright, open, a level playing field.

On the day that Sandra graduated from university, Glen had closed the restaurant, which otherwise happened only at Christmas. Marilyn had taken the day off work and had even insisted that Walter attend. To Sandra's embarrassment, her mother had hired a photographer. Sandra knew that for her family she was a source of mixed feelings, a frog who couldn't decide to live on land or swim in water; she was an object of love, pride and jealousy. She was the only one born in Canada and because of that they continued to call her the *hoo sung*. Especially Marilyn. Marilyn was nine when she arrived in Canada and Glen was thirteen. Glen went to school for a few years, but quit after grade eight. Marilyn graduated from the four year commercial course in high school. She worked for a while as a bank teller before marrying Walter. Her marriage to Walter had been considered a real triumph, a step into true white-collar middle-class life. But it was achieved through marriage, whereas Sandra was a member of the professional class because of her education. She was the one who moved with total ease through Canadian life. Her track was smooth and straight; she never stumbled. It wasn't that Glen and Marilyn hadn't been blessed. It was just that Sandra had been blessed more. Their envy was never overwhelming. It came out obliquely, good-naturedly. They bragged to others about Sandra's university degree, but then quickly added how much greater their accomplishments would be had they only had the same opportunities. Glen was always a highly paid engineer, building fantastic bridges and roads. And Marilyn would be a lawyer, faithfully serving the Chinese community.

But gradually Sandra began to appreciate her position of ignorance. Not knowing, not being able to negotiate her way around the intricacies of Chinese social behaviour, gave her protection. No one really held her accountable. She was not taken as a serious player in the game of family politics and diplomacy.

Sandra got up from the couch and walked stiffly to the bathroom. She brushed her teeth, then she splashed cold water on her face.

The next day, Sandra spent her lunch hour pouring over the blank cards at Eaton's. She spent the next two nights rewriting the invitations to the Chinese guests on cards with two birds on the cover. She wasn't going to be responsible for a curse on anybody's life.

The parents of Sandra's best friend, Gail, lived in a large spacious house in the Kingsway. They generously agreed to hold the reception in their home. There was a magnificent foyer with a winding staircase. The living room was filled with overstuffed couches and chairs covered in flowered chintz. The bay window overlooked a hedge of spirea. The dining room opened onto a cedar deck that in the summer flowed into smooth green lawns and beds of roses. But it was the middle of March and the backyard was covered with melting piles of darkly speckled granular snow. The flowering shrubs looked bare and skeletal.

Sandra and Victor wanted a simple reception of wine, beer and hors d'oeuvres. On the day of the reception, everything looked perfect. The dining table was covered with a thick white damask tablecloth, with a centrepiece of elegant white calla lilies. There were vases of flowers everywhere —

yellow and white lilies, blue irises, many coloured snapdragons. The waiters were ready in their black trousers and vests and white shirts. A small folk group with a singer, guitar player and violinist provided sweet, gentle music. Sandra was eager to show her family that she, the little sister, really did know how to pull off a big social affair. She even made sure that there were nibbles like deep fried wontons, chicken and shrimp satays, so that the Chinese guests would be comfortable with the food.

Sandra squeezed Victor's hand as she surveyed the surroundings. She was pleased with what she saw. People gradually started to arrive. Everything appeared to be going smoothly. Their friends and Victor's family arrived first. Then Sandra's relatives started to slowly trickle in. Her nieces and nephews who were all Canadian-born, warmly but quickly, greeted her and Victor, before attaching themselves to the buffet table.

Marilyn, all smiles, rushed over and gave Victor a quick peck on the cheek. She put her arm around Sandra and beamed at her in her special loving big-sisterly way. "Well done, Sandra. Very high-class. Walter and I have been to parties like this before, you know. The *lo fons* will love it." Then she took Walter's arm and they started mingling. Sandra turned to Victor and grinned. She heard Marilyn speaking on the other side of the room. "I'm the bride's sister. My husband, Walter.... What do we do?... Oh, we have a bookkeeping company. Very small, not much business," as she gestured with her left hand, a large diamond and emerald ring glittering on her wedding finger.

Out of the corner of her eye Sandra caught a glimpse of Glen and May looking at the buffet table. Her brother was wearing a suit that probably hadn't been worn in fifteen years. There was something about the way they were huddling and whispering that immediately sent waves of uncertainty through Sandra's body. Glen ate three bowls of steamed rice at every meal. He stared in disbelief at the trays of tiny nibbles that were being offered.

Suddenly Sandra's mother was standing next to her, taking her aside. Her body stiffened as she listened to her mother's hoarse whisper. "Sanda-*ah*, Sanda-*ah*. You have too many white flowers. For the Chinese, white is the colour of death. You should've checked with me first. And don't you know that Chinese people expect to come to a sit-down banquet. *Eiiyah*! People are going to think you're stingy. Take their gifts and give them so little to eat."

For the rest of the reception, Sandra found herself acutely aware of all the conversation. Every voice seemed magnified. There was lavish praise. "What a lovely reception. Great place. Great food." And there were uncomfortable whispers and furtive glances. "What's this? Is this all we're eating?"

Throughout it all, Sandra remained the perfectly composed bride. But her palms grew clammy and her stomach tightened as she realized the extent of her social blunder. Her ignorance of Chinese traditions had until now been grudgingly forgiven, considered even a part of her charm. But marriage was a major life decision. By not doing things properly, she was tempting fate. She knew that her mother would be phoning.

Three weeks later, Mrs Low held a dinner in honour of her daughter's marriage to Victor. It was a nine-course, sit-down banquet at a Chinese restaurant. Sandra arrived in a long-sleeved shift of red fluid silk. Around her neck she wore a large jade pendant on a heavy gold chain, a gift from her mother. All the Chinese guests were invited, along with Victor's family. For good luck, there were plates of oranges. There were bowls of steaming shark's fin soup, lobster with ginger, crispy-skin chicken, delicate stir-fried scallops with smoky mushrooms, noodles for long life, and more. In the middle of each round table proudly stood a bottle of *Johnny Walker Red Label* Scotch, for more good luck.

Mrs Low, wearing a rose-coloured brocade suit, led Sandra and Victor from table to table, offering their welcome to all the guests. Mrs Yee, the matchmaker, was sitting at the first table. She turned and smiled at Mrs Low, Sandra and Victor. Then she looked directly at Mrs Low, "You must be so happy. Finally, Sandra married. *Lo fons* not all bad, you know...."

Mrs Low was prepared. "Oh, you know young people today. They want to decide themselves. *Lo fons* aren't all bad, just like Chinese aren't all good. The good thing, though — *half-and-half* children are the most beautiful. They have the best of both worlds."

Mrs Yee nodded in agreement. "Nothing we can do about it if young people want to choose themselves." She shrugged her shoulders. "My daughter is going with a *lo fon*. As long as you have a good son-in-law. Doesn't matter Chinese or *lo fon*."

Mrs Low relaxed a little and smiled. "Well, you know, people pay money for his paintings. He can do so much around the house. Very hard-working, good with his hands. And he loves Chinese food, even the fermented black beans. He even uses chopsticks like a Chinaman. If you can get a son-in-law like that, *lo fon* is okay."

Sandra was grateful that Victor didn't understand Chinese. She smiled to herself at the irony of those comments. Only a few months ago, her mother was calling Victor that *gwei loh*, that devil man. Now she was touting him as the catch of the century. But as they exchanged greetings with guests, table after table, Sandra couldn't help but notice the tightly stitched smile on her mother's face and the words occasionally catching in her throat. When she returned to the head table, she opened her palm and saw that she was clutching several red lucky money envelopes, pressed into her hand by the older Chinese guests while she was making the rounds. Sandra unzipped a secret pocket in the back of her purse and carefully placed the gifts of luck inside.

6

THE GOOD LUCK CAFÉ

THE NIGHT JOHNNY SUE FELL FROM THE THIRD FLOOR OF HIS restaurant was like any other night. After he and his son, Tony, closed the dining room and cleaned up, Tony went to bed. Johnny went up to the roof with a bottle of Scotch. Nobody knew whether he fell or leaped. When a cop found him at four in the morning, he had to bang for more than twenty minutes on the restaurant door to wake Tony up. Everyone thought he must have died right away after falling three floors, but nobody knew for sure. How long had he lain there? Was he moaning?

When Tony saw his father's body in a crumpled heap on the sidewalk, he was unable to utter a single sound. When he finally found his voice, the words erupted in a stammer, like the rapid teeth-tapping of a trapped animal. The stutter remained for the rest of his life. Sometimes it diminished but it never entirely left — a rat gnawing inside his throat.

After the funeral, Tony called the real estate agent and left town. Nothing was disturbed; nothing touched. Upstairs there were three bedrooms, two of them facing the brick wall of the furniture store. The room at the front looked across the road to the Urquhart bus station. Each room had a single bed with a twisted wire frame and a narrow mattress, covered with thin sheets and moth-eaten blankets. In the front room there was a chest of drawers with a splotchy mirror. Downstairs, everything remained ready for business. A few ashtrays needed to be emptied, but the cooler was stocked with milk and cream. The refrigerator was filled with hamburger patties, strips of halibut, iceberg lettuce, cole slaw and bean sprouts. Jammed in the back were egg rolls, breaded chicken balls and breaded spare ribs, all partly cooked and ready for the deep fryer, though the place stood empty. The stained walls, the ceiling tiles and the very air smelled of stale tobacco, rotting food, and death.

Tony was expecting the cafe to stay empty for several months. He expected a *lo fon*, someone who didn't believe in Chinese superstitions, to buy the place. He was surprised when the real estate agent brought him an offer from two Chinese brothers.

Eight years before Johnny Sue's death, the Lee brothers, Eddie and Jimmy, had arrived in Canada. Eddie, the older brother, chose to go to Toronto to wait on tables for his uncle's restaurant, The Carlaw Cafe. He lived upstairs on the second floor with three other waiters and two cooks. Every day for eight years, Eddie put on his loose black pants and white cotton waiter's jacket, walked up and down the aisle of the restaurant, and served the guests seated inside the row of wooden booths, carrying plates of grilled cheese sandwiches, hot beef sandwiches, sweet and sour spare ribs and combination plates one, two and three. On his days off, Eddie went to the Rose Garden Theatre and watched the movie screen fill with stars from Hong Kong. Mesmerized by their lives of wealth and drama, he sat cracking roasted watermelon seeds between his teeth, carefully collecting the shells in his hands, while those around him spat their shells on the floor.

Jimmy found a position as an apprentice cook in a Chinese restaurant in a small town outside Windsor. There he learned to cook grilled cheese sandwiches, hot beef sandwiches, sweet and sour spare ribs and combination plates one, two and three — the identical dishes that his brother carried more than two hundred miles away.

When Eddie found out about Johnny Sue's restaurant, he immediately recognized an opportunity. He could already see himself seated behind the cash register, taking the money from the customers, while his brother did the cooking in the back. Eddie and Jimmy bargained a third off the asking price and closed the deal in three weeks. When they finally got the key and opened the door to the restaurant, they looked around, then at each other and nodded with satisfaction.

Jimmy cleaned and scrubbed out the refrigerator, throwing out the trays of rotten meat and bundles of soggy deteriorating vegetables, while Eddie poured gallons of sour milk down the drains. Jimmy polished the tables and painted the walls. Eddie filled out the orders for fresh supplies. He washed out the ash trays and the glass sugar dispensers. When each container was dry, he filled it with fresh sugar and screwed on the shiny silver-coloured, conical-shaped lids. Here was a chance to work for themselves, to be independent at last. Their luck had finally changed. They understood their good fortune. Yet it remained unspoken.

Even after a new red and green electric sign was swinging outside at right angles to the storefront; even after the restaurant was renamed the Good Luck Cafe, they remembered the stench of rotting meat that greeted them when they first opened the double refrigerator doors. They remembered the way Johnny had died and the legacy in Tony's stutter.

There were two other Chinese restaurants in Urquhart. Eddie and Jimmy were surprised when, on opening day, each of them sent a large potted plant festooned with red ribbons and a red envelope. A few days later, when Eddie walked over to the Golden Gate Restaurant and the China Palace Cafe, he understood the acts of generosity. The restaurants were *goh-sheng*, high class like the Sai Woo and Kwongchow in Toronto. His restaurant across from the bus station was no threat. As Eddie chatted with Bill Woo, the owner of the Golden Gate, he looked at the large room divider decorated with a golden dragon and phoenix. Eddie sipped at his coffee and nibbled at a tiny delicate almond cookie. He looked at Bill. His full-cheeked smiling face and confidence made Eddie feel welcomed and humbled at the same time.

Eddie liked managing the dining room, giving the clients the impression that he was the sole owner. He liked pulling down the handle of the cash register and hearing the drawer spring out, then taking the money from the customers, while his brother worked with his hands in the kitchen. For Eddie though, owning the Good Luck Cafe meant more than just being a boss. He was anxious to get married and begin a family. He was thirty-two and Jimmy was thirty. Each was desperate to relieve the aching throb that persisted between his legs. Eddie realized that with his new status as a boss and entrepreneur, his chances of acquiring a desirable mail-order bride were much greater. In the past, whenever he visited a matchmaker, the pictures he saw of the girls willing to marry someone who was just an employee were less attractive. The girls were a little on the dumpy side, their skin a little pock-marked. The Good Luck Cafe was his chance to be like his uncle and sit like a boss at the cash register, to get a wife, to lose his virginity. Who knew the real story about Johnny Sue, the brothers asked each other? Who knew whether Johnny Sue's death was an accident or suicide? Did he really leave the place cursed? Who cared? Probably — if at all — only Johnny Sue's son, Tony Sue, cared. After all, these superstitions belonged in China, not Canada.

Six months after the opening of the Good Luck Cafe, Aunt Lucy visited her friend Mrs. Yee, the matchmaker, and found a mail-order bride from Hong Kong for Eddie. Lucy showed him a picture of a broad-faced young woman with round eyes and a high forehead. The prospective bride wrote and said that she was five feet tall and weighed 100 pounds, that she had gone to high school for two years, had two brothers and two sisters and was nineteen years old. Now, one year later, Eddie stood in the arrival lounge at the airport in Toronto with his brother, Jimmy, Aunt Lucy and Uncle George. He stood with a rolled up Chinese newspaper under one arm. Yu Ling's picture he held in one hand, while the other was in his jacket pocket, turning over in his fingers a small pink silk-covered jewellery box. Eddie craned his neck in various directions as he tried to find a face in the crowd that matched the picture in his hand.

Walking from the plane into the crowded airport, Yu Ling Wong had never felt terror like this. It surprised her. She knew that right now, if someone lunged at her out of nowhere, she would not utter a sound. Her legs had not gone rubbery, as she had thought they might. Instead they felt rigid, like sticks and she could barely move one in front of the other. She clutched her bag so tightly that the strap stretched taut over her shoulder. Yu Ling had never seen so many *lo fons* before, though she was not unfamiliar with them. In Hong Kong she had seen them in their police uniforms, and the ones from India, wearing turbans around their heads.

When she left the plane she followed the stream of passengers. What if they fanned out in different directions? Who would she follow? the large woman with the brightly flowered printed dress who sat beside her and ate the serving of cubed fruit in a clear, too-sweet syrup that Yu Ling didn't want? or the middle-aged man with long stringy strands of hair carefully combed over his bald head? For the moment, she felt safe. She stood and blinked under white lights, surrounded and held upright by bodies, barely able to see over their shoulders, staring into chests and armpits, feeling that any moment she would vaporize into a thicket of coats and towering bodies.

Everyone around her seemed confident, had a sense of purpose as they craned their necks, knowing which face to look for, then the sudden recognition — outstretched arms, laughter, tears and talk. As the crowd thinned, the terror in Yu Ling's body turned into panic. Then she saw him. *Oh God! He looks just like the pictures. His ears sticking out at right angles. And his chin looks stubborn. He's shorter than I thought he'd be.* Yu Ling surprised herself with these thoughts. And then she remembered *This is the man I'm supposed to marry.* When Eddie finally saw her, a slow smile spread across his face. *Oh my! That's why his lips were closed in every picture.* The teeth were large and misshapen, growing one on top of the other. Her tongue automatically glided over her own perfectly-shaped, even teeth.

Eddie nodded in nervous recognition as he started to walk toward Yu Ling. He looked down and noticed that she was wearing shiny black high heels. *I wonder if she's really five feet tall.* Eddie was dressed in an ill-fitting brown suit. His hand fidgeted with the roll of Chinese newspaper. His brother Jimmy, half a head taller, stood beside him. He was dressed in a brown suit like Eddie's, loose and ill-fitting. But there was something different about the body inside. You could sense the lithe muscles, alert, tense, ready to pounce. By the time Yu Ling noticed Jimmy, he had already looked her over, taken her in.

Eddie stood and blinked at Yu Ling. She stood solidly before him, no longer a black-and-white two dimensional image on a shiny piece of paper. This woman he would marry and live with. Abruptly, Aunt Lucy stepped forward and said, "You must be Wong Yu Ling." Yu Ling nodded with a frozen smile on her face. "I am Auntie Lucy. This is Uncle George, Eddie, your husband-to-be, and Jimmy, his brother."

Yu Ling kept smiling as she remembered what one of her girlfriends had said to her, "Whatever you do, don't let them name you Lucy. In Chinese it sounds too much like mouse, or worse, loosing your shit."

Eddie took a step closer to Yu Ling. "Was everything all right?" And he handed to her the pink square box from his jacket pocket. Inside was a bracelet made of five gold petals.

Each was engraved with a letter to make up the word H.A.P.P.Y.

Yu Ling arrived in Canada on Thursday. She and Eddie would be married on Sunday. Eddie remembered sitting with Lucy in the living room of Mrs Yee, the matchmaker. She lived on the first floor of a semi-detached house on Dundas Street in Toronto. Eddie could smell the barbecued meat from the restaurant next door. He was surprised by the age of the matchmaker. He had expected an older woman, someone in her fifties. Instead, he and Lucy were greeted at the door by a woman in her mid-thirties. Lucy handed her a box filled with barbecued pork, steamed buns and egg tarts. As Mrs Yee led them down a narrow, windowless hallway, she held a baby, noisily sucking from a bottle. The floor was covered with a long piece of scratched-up linoleum, randomly patterned in gold paisley. The room at the end of the hall was cluttered with cardboard boxes of various sizes and shapes stacked in wobbly looking piles. Lining the window ledge were jars of different sizes and shapes, each filled with shiny beads and sequins. On a smoky pink couch rested a stack of woollen sweaters in the process of being decorated in intricate, iridescent patterns with the beads and sequins. A matching armchair was jammed in a corner, facing the couch. In between was a wooden coffee table.

They sat down and discussed the date of the wedding. "Should we wait a week or two before getting married — so that she has a chance to get settled?" Eddie asked.

"Tsk! Don't be so naive," Lucy responded immediately. "You need to get married as soon as possible. You don't want to give her a chance to change her mind."

"Oh?"

Mrs Yee poured three cups of jasmine tea and explained. "Well, there have been cases of brides refusing to go through with the marriage." Eddie was now listening intently. "I know of one case where the bride ran away."

Lucy interrupted, "She's arriving on a Thursday. She can stay with me and Uncle George until Sunday."

"On Friday she can be fitted for a gown. I'll ask my cousin to take her. Her English is not bad. If you pay them a little extra, they'll have the gown ready."

Lucy nodded with approval. Eddie sighed with relief and sipped his tea. Mrs Yee continued, "Do you want my oldest girl to be the flower girl? You won't have to buy a dress. The one she wore at the last ceremony still fits her. I'll have to buy her new shoes, though. The old ones don't fit any more."

"Yes, that would be good," said Lucy.

"Yes, thank you for all your trouble," added Eddie, setting his cup on the coffee table.

When Eddie and Lucy got up to leave, he tickled the baby under the chin and tucked a red envelope under its arm. Inside, there was enough money to make the matchmaker's efforts worth her while and to pay for a child's new pair of shoes.

For Yu Ling the wedding was a blur. There was a general feeling of mild, but persistent discomfort. It had to do with the wedding gown. The day after Yu Ling arrived, Aunt Lucy and the matchmaker's cousin took her to Syd Silver's. The *lo fon* saleslady looked at her and frowned. She turned smartly on her high heels and marched to a special corner of the store. When she returned, she was holding a white gown in one arm and a veil in the other. "This is the smallest dress we have. But don't worry, I can make it fit." The matchmaker's cousin led Yu Ling to the dressing room. When Yu Ling returned, she stood shapeless and helpless in front of a full length mirror, drowning in mountainous folds of shiny white satin. Stiff circular layers of netting stuck out sharply from her head. The saleslady smiled sweetly, armed with a box of straight pins. "No problem, dear. WE can make this fit." Her fingers deftly lifted the shoulders of the dress and pinned in new seams. The corners of her mouth were turned down in grim determination as she clutched the back seam to show how a few strategic nips would make the whole thing fit. "We'll make this look like it was made for you." Then she folded back a few layers of the netting on Yu Ling's head. "See how perfectly it frames your face now." The saleslady stood back slightly to admire her work. She then looked at Aunt Lucy who nodded with satisfaction.

Two days later, at the wedding reception, Yu Ling stared at the faces of the guests and could only think about the armholes feeling too tight and the starched netting chafing at her forehead. The back seam was too thick and rubbed at the base of her neck.

Then there was the clanging of the spoons. It always started out a few at a time, against the glasses filled with Scotch, or soft drink, or tea. Once it started, it never faded, building up decibel by decibel to a crescendo. As Eddie shyly stole a glance at Yu Ling, they rose stiffly, their bodies rigid as they leaned toward each other, their lips barely brushing — the people at the reception taking sadistic, good-natured glee in their awkward embarrassment. There was not a single person who did not know they had never even held hands, much less kissed. And yet strangely, it was this that brought them together, more than the marriage ceremony. Not the kissing, but the clanging roar of spoons, forcing them into a narrower, deeper corner — and the audience, it was starting to feel like an audience, crowding in on them. Uncle George with his face red and glowing, Aunt Lucy nodding with brisk satisfaction and Jimmy, catching and holding Yu Ling's stare as he noisily sucked on a fat lobster leg and then roughly wiped his lips, leaving them red and slightly swollen. The sea of faces locked her into position with Eddie, leaving no choice, no escape, her soul cleaving to his, not out of love, but fear.

Jimmy walked into the dining room of the Good Luck Cafe, triumphantly carrying a dish of gently stir-fried succulent scallops with smoky dried mushrooms. He placed it in front of Yu Ling, who smiled with delight. "Ah, Jimmy, this smells wonderful. You shouldn't have gone to so much trouble."

"No problem, very easy, Ling *soh*," replied Jimmy, calling her, respectfully, sister-in-law, as he picked up his ceramic spoon and dipped it into the large bowl of winter melon soup. His eyes remained fixed on his sister-in-law's face.

Yu Ling picked up a plump, shiny scallop between her chopsticks and popped it into her mouth. "Ummmm. Perfect!" She sighed in appreciation, smiling and returning Jimmy's gaze.

Eddie scowled and muttered under his breath, steadily watching his brother and his wife. "Shrimps yesterday, lobster the night before. Show-off. Who's he trying to impress?"

Eddie picked up one of the scallops with his chopsticks and popped it in his mouth. "Not enough salt."

From the very beginning, Eddie understood his younger brother's interest in his new wife. It wasn't easy living all those years without a woman. Eddie enjoyed flaunting his new status as a husband, as someone who had finally experienced a woman. Every night, he was aware of Jimmy's footsteps, how they stopped outside their bedroom door. Eddie would pump harder and harder into Yu Ling's body, so the springs of their bed would squeak louder and louder — if only to let Jimmy know what he was missing.

But then Eddie started to notice small changes in Jimmy's behaviour. Every morning, Yu Ling came down to the dining room at about 10:30 to help prepare for the opening of the restaurant at eleven. She entered the room just as the announcer at the bus station across the street finished calling the route: "Durham, Chatsworth ... Owen Sound." She walked over to the counter to wash the dirty glasses from the previous evening. There was a row of three stainless steel sinks and a draining rack. First, she placed the dirty glasses in the sink to her right. The middle one she filled with hot soapy water, and the third one with clear hot water and a capful of bleach. Every morning Jimmy rushed out from the kitchen. "Ah, good morning, Ling *soh*. Let me help you get these dried."

"That's very kind of you, Jimmy, but really, I can manage. You must have lots to do in the kitchen."

"Not much left to do there. It'll be much faster if I help you."

In his corner of the dining room, Eddie filled the rows of tiny china coffee creamers and the glass sugar dispensers.

His hands worked mechanically, automatically, as his eyes locked in the direction of his wife and his brother — absorbing the image of his brother squeezing between the counter and Yu Ling, noticing his brother's thighs brush against the body of his wife, and a few moments later, watching as their fingertips accidentally touched and Yu Ling smiling, shyly, in response.

Yu Ling never was able to get from Jimmy the details of what really happened. That night, after the restaurant closed, she went upstairs to run a bath. There was a dull persistent ache in her back, and the swelling in her calves and feet made her shoes feel small and tight. She left Jimmy tidying up in the kitchen. In the dining room Eddie was counting the cash.

Eddie was especially proud of the furniture in their bedroom. It was almost as good as what he imagined the *lo fons* to have. He had bought, second hand, two matching wooden chests of drawers, and a metal double bed with a wire frame. The mattress he bought new.

Yu Ling walked to her dresser and pulled out the small top drawer that contained her underwear. Reaching into the back, she felt the gold coin that Jimmy had given her for Chinese New Year. She remembered how he waited until Eddie had left the kitchen. He had pressed it into her hand, wrapping his fingers around her fist with the gold piece inside. It seemed such an extravagant gift from a brother-in-law. Without a word being spoken, Yu Ling understood immediately that Eddie didn't know, was not meant to know. As she held the coin in her fingers, Yu Ling remembered the warmth of Jimmy's hand surrounding her own.

Yu Ling closed the drawer, breathed deeply and let out a long breath of air, walked over to the window that overlooked the bus station. It wasn't that she hadn't thought of running away. She knew that Eddie kept a roll of bills in the left pocket of his pants, which he hung every night on the hook on the back of the bedroom door. But where would she go? She didn't even know the words necessary for buying a ticket. Yu Ling sighed and pulled the blind down over the window.

She slowly undressed, put on her housecoat and placed her neatly folded clothes on a wooden chair next to the bed. Then she crossed the hall and filled the bathtub with hot water. Leaving her housecoat in a heap on the floor, she carefully stepped into the tub, gently easing herself into the water. The porcelain-enamelled, cast-iron tub stood on four clawed feet. It was long enough to allow Yu Ling to rest her head against the back and stretch out. She waved her arms gently in the water, making waves that lapped soothingly over her body. The heat seeped into her pores, loosening the knots in her calves and the muscles in the small of her back. Yu Ling tilted back her head and stared at the flaking paint on the ceiling. She closed her eyes, rested her hands on her slightly swollen belly and breathed slowly and deeply. This was the only thing about Canada that she really liked. In Hong Kong she had to heat water on a gas stove and pour it into a round galvanized steel tub. That tub had only been large enough for squatting. Here, the restaurant had an unlimited supply of hot water. Yu Ling felt like a queen as she relaxed in a sea of heat.

Yu Ling thought back to her third day in Urquhart, when Eddie had taken her to visit the Golden Gate

Restaurant. The weather had been warm and Yu Ling was wearing a flower-printed dress. There was just enough breeze to make the soft cotton of her dress cling to her, gently outlining the roundness of her breasts and the fullness of her hips. Mrs Woo clasped Yu Ling's hand in hers. "Oh, here comes the bride, here comes the bride. You must be very happy Eddie *Sook*."

Eddie smiled nervously. They sat down with the Woos for tea and almond biscuits. "How's business?" asked Eddie.

"Oh, so-so," said Mr Woo. But Eddy knew better. It wasn't polite to brag and tell the truth.

Mr Woo looked at Yu Ling, then lifted one eyebrow higher than the other and turned to Eddie. "You're lucky to have such a *beautiful* bride," smirking ever so slightly.

Eddie's jaw tensed and his eyes flashed angrily. He forced out the words, "So-so." He knew it wasn't polite to agree and brag. Mrs Woo was heavy and thick set.

"And soon there'll be lots of children," added Mrs Woo quickly.

Yu Ling blushed as Mr Woo looked at her. She looked at Eddie and saw his face turning rigid like a mask, his eyes glittering with anger. Suddenly he got up and said to her, "We must go now. We need to get back to work."

"Oh so soon?" said Mrs Woo, smiling, looking puzzled. "You don't need to go so soon. Stay some more."

"Thank you very much for your hospitality," said Eddie stiffly.

"Yes, yes, thank you," said Yu Ling. She wanted to add "Be sure to visit us soon," but did not dare.

"Well, come and visit again." said Mr Woo.

Eddie marched briskly out of the restaurant. Yu Ling

rushed to catch up. "Eddie, why are you in such a hurry?"

"Didn't you see the way he looked at you? Full of salty, lewd thoughts."

"But he was just being friendly. Really complimenting you, not me."

"You don't know anything." Eddie stared straight ahead. He walked so quickly, Yu Ling could barely keep up.

That was their only visit to the Golden Gate Restaurant together; and Eddie never took her to the China Palace Cafe, as he had once promised. As a matter of fact, she rarely stepped out of the restaurant. Once, three months after their visit with the Woos, Eddie took her to a store that sounded like Wah-kar. There he bought her a navy blue winter coat. That was the last time she had left the restaurant.

Seven days a week they worked in the restaurant and at night they went upstairs to sleep. On Tuesday nights, the Chinese grocery truck made its regular weekly stop at the Good Luck. Jimmy always ordered Chinese food supplies for the kitchen. Once he made a point of asking Yu Ling, "What would you like to eat? If you tell me, I'll order it for next week." When she turned to reply she noticed that Jimmy was staring at his brother.

Every few weeks, Eddie allowed her to buy a Chinese movie magazine from the grocery truck. Yu Ling was pleased with the chance to talk to someone other than the brothers. But Eddie always interrupted the conversation and the grocer was in a hurry to get back to Toronto.

The water in the tub was beginning to cool. She leaned forward and turned on the hot water tap.

Jimmy and Eddie had been fighting so much recently. Mostly over little things, like food orders being filled too slowly. It was always Eddie losing his temper with Jimmy. And it happened again tonight. Jimmy had steamed a bass with ginger and scallions. The flesh was firm and delicately flavoured. But again Eddie had found fault. "This fish is over-cooked. The flesh is all mushy. You call yourself a cook. Good thing you don't cook for Chinese. Only *lo fons* would be fooled by your cooking."

Yu Ling had tried to soften Eddie's words. "But the fish is very nice. Try another piece." And she smiled apologetically at Jimmy whose left fist was clenched, hidden from view under the table.

She knew Jimmy's partnership was important to the restaurant. Anybody could be a waiter, but a good cook was hard to find. It was true that Jimmy had been paying Yu Ling a lot of attention, more than was right from a brother-in-law. He noticed little things — that she preferred fish to meat, that she had a love of clear soups and fresh fruit. The fact that he had bothered to notice made her feel, if not special, at least worthwhile, and perhaps, a little less alone. But was there more to it? The heat from the bath had put her in a kind of trance. In a strange way it was helping her to slowly, gradually see. What was the real reason for Jimmy's kindness? Sometimes she caught him looking at her in a way that was unnerving, yet thrilling. And she knew that Eddie found her body appealing. Even in her condition he wanted to do it — sometimes two or even three times a night. He wanted to possess her, swallow her up. Yu Ling smiled to herself. A short, sharp laugh burst from her throat. Deep down, she was realizing how much she liked not only the attention, but the intrigue — that dark surge of exhilaration. She smiled again; then without warning she started to weep.

Yu Ling leaned back against the bathtub with her eyes shut, trying to block out the arguing voices from the floor below. Then a scream rose out of the muffled angry rumble. The muscles in her body tensed. Feeling gripped with fear, she leaped out of the tub, awkwardly pulled on her cotton housecoat, half-stumbled down the stairs and pushed past the door into the kitchen. Her heart stopped. Jimmy was sobbing as he crouched beside his brother who was slumped on the floor with a slash in his throat, his face in a pool of blood. Yu Ling stood in the kitchen doorway and stared at the bloody knife that laid on the floor beside her husband's head. Her hand covered her mouth, stifling the horror that filled her body.

Jimmy turned to Yu Ling. They stared at each other for a long moment before he spoke. "It all happened so quickly. He blamed you for everything. Accused me of sleeping with you. Then came at me with the cleaver." Jimmy could barely control his sobbing. "I picked up the knife when he came at me. The next thing I knew, I had stabbed him in the throat."

"I-I can't believe this." Yu Ling clutched her swollen belly. Looking around, she saw that the wooden barrel holding the dirty cutlery, had been knocked over onto its side. Knives and forks and spoons lay scattered all over the floor, glistening in a pool of weak sudsy water. She stood staring at Eddie on the floor.

"What am I going to do?" Jimmy blurted.

Yu Ling continued to stare at him, saying nothing, unable to move. The garbage stood unemptied. She smelled the rotting meat and the decaying vegetables, mingling with a trace of shampoo in her freshly washed hair, still wet on her shoulders. She stood peeling back the layers of a trance, waking from a stupor, waking into a nightmare. She turned and ran back upstairs.

The coat that Eddie had bought her three months before was somewhere in her closet. Find it. Put it on. She had to leave. When Yu Ling stepped out of the Good Luck she was surprised by the chill of the winter air and automatically wrapped her unbuttoned coat more tightly around her body. She looked up and saw, suspended in the dark cloudless sky, a sharp crescent moon, translucent as rice paper. Without thinking, she knew where to go. Her face was streaked with tears as she banged on the door, then the window, then the door, the window. When Mr Woo unlocked the door of the Golden Gate, Yu Ling looked down and saw the corduroy bedroom slippers on her feet.

The police came and took Jimmy away. He got off. Self-defence. Yu Ling stayed with the Woos until The Good Luck was sold. Months later, she and her newborn daughter moved into a rooming house in Toronto's Chinatown. A short while later she found work in a sewing factory and later bought a tiny house on Glasgow Street. She lived downstairs with her daughter and rented the three rooms upstairs. Three years later she met and married a man with a stutter and fear in his eyes. A man named Tony Sue.

7

THE GHOST WIFE

O NCE IN LONG-AGO CHINA THERE LIVED A YOUNG FARMER WHO, although he worked hard, barely made enough to eat. When it came time for him to marry, no family wanted their daughter to marry someone with such meagre prospects.

Every day, on his way home he walked past a wood. One evening, as he was returning home after tending the fields, he saw, standing next to a tree, someone he had never seen before. It was a young woman and she was weeping. When the farmer learned that she was lost, he agreed to take her to the crossroads, a short distance from her home. When they got there, the farmer watched as she moved away from him, her slim figure growing dimmer and dimmer in the twilight until she disappeared.

For the next few days, the young farmer could think of no one else. At times, when he looked up from his work in the fields, he thought he saw her, a distant ephemeral presence. Each evening as he walked past the woods, he looked to see if perhaps she was between the trees.

One night, after the farmer had finished his chores and was preparing for bed, he heard a knock. When he opened the door, he saw standing before him, the young woman who had been lost.

"If you will have me, I will be your wife. I bring with me no dowry, but I promise that while we are together we will never go hungry." The young woman spoke in a voice barely above a whisper. Once again the farmer marvelled at her beauty. She was slender and graceful, with a complexion so pale that it was almost translucent.

"Yes," said the farmer. "Yes, I wish to have you for my wife."

"But there is one condition," said the young woman. "Promise me that once we are married, at night when we are in bed and asleep, you will never light a candle and gaze upon my form."

Although this request seemed strange, it also seemed a simple request to fulfil. The farmer agreed.

The farmer and his young wife lived happily together for several years. Just as the young woman had promised, the farmer began to enjoy bountiful harvests. He never felt hungry again. Finally, he even had enough vegetables left over to take to market.

When the farmer arrived at the market, however, the villagers greeted him with dismay. There was concern in their voices. "How thin and pale you look!" The farmer was puzzled. He had never felt better. His stomach was always full and his fields were overflowing. When he returned home and told his wife, she said, "Pay them no attention. They are just jealous of your good fortune. You have enough food here. There is no need for you to return to the village."

But the words of the villagers echoed in his head, and twice the farmer returned to the market. And each time the villagers remarked on his appearance and asked if his wife had fed him enough?

Finally, he decided to visit a pond in a neighbouring farmer's field. He knelt down at the edge of the pond and peered at his reflection. He barely recognized himself. His skin was grey, his cheeks hollowed, his eyes sunken and his shoulders bony. Yet when he looked at his arms in the sunlight, they were tanned and well muscled. When his fingers touched his cheeks, they felt full and firm. But when he once again examined his reflection in the water, he was shocked by what he saw.

When he returned home that evening, he related what he saw to his wife. Her eyes were alarmed, but she spoke reassuringly. "Your eyes must have been playing a trick on you. Why, you yourself said that you had never felt better." And she begged him, "Do not go back to the village. Stay here with me where you are happy."

But the farmer said nothing. He grew silent and suspicious. He remembered what his wife had told him — that at night when she was asleep, he was never to light a candle and look upon her form.

That night he decided that he could stand it no longer. He was determined to see his wife's true form. He pretended to fall asleep beside her. When her breathing became slow and deep, the farmer rose from his bed. He reached for the candle and lit it.

When he saw the form before him, he fainted and dropped the flame. The bed caught fire and the flames spread to the rest of the cottage. In the morning, when the villagers came, they found a smouldering shell of a home. Inside, on the remnants of a bed, they found a badly charred body. Beside it was a skeleton. Long black hair was attached to the skull. The bones glistened white in the sunlight.

My mother told me this story many times during my childhood. I was always repelled and lured at the same time, like peering into a deep dark well, wanting to see clear to the bottom, yet fearful of falling in.

We were inside Timothy Eaton United Church for Jean Woo's wedding. There must have been at least a thousand people, all there to see Jean take her nuptial vows. I stood between my parents. My father was dressed in a dark blue, light wool suit with his hands loosely clasped in front of him. His relaxed, self-contained presence was always in stark contrast to my mother. Today it seemed even more so. I looked at the shimmer of my mother's raw silk suit. She had chosen a plum colour because it flattered her complexion. Or so the saleswoman told her.

Her hair was a pretty cloud of intense black curls, those betraying white roots having been banished the previous day by the hairdresser. My mother and I strained to see the procession as it moved slowly down the aisle.

There were six bridesmaids, a flower girl and a ring bearer. Each girl was dressed in a matching Laura Ashley print, with a full skirt and with a large bow in the small of the back. Jean's gown was a gentle combination of soft silk and lace. Her headdress was a single layer of fine tulle attached to a wreath of white and pink roses. The church was overflowing with flowers — expensive looking arrangements from a North Toronto florist. Jean's taste had come a long way from Urquhart, the small city where we both grew up.

My mother's face was tense as she arched her back and craned her neck. I noticed an almost indiscernible twitch underneath her left eye and her lips barely moved as she silently counted the attendants. She had not expected Jean to get married before me. She had always assumed that I would be first.

Jean and I had attended Urquhart Collegiate together. After high school, Jean went to train as a paediatric nurse at the Hospital for Sick Children in Toronto. To my mother's pride and dismay, I went to university and majored in English. While I was finishing my last year, Jean had already been nursing for a year, making a decent salary for a young woman in 1975. To make matters worse, I had just declared that I intended to continue my education and had no job prospect in sight.

There were two Chinese restaurants in Urquhart. Ours, and the Woo's. There was a third, but it didn't count. It was a family business, had no hired labour, the local greasy spoon. Our restaurant, the China Palace Cafe was smaller than the Woo's, but it was classier. It had white tablecloths and the waiters wore burgundy red jackets. My mother had imported several Chinese silk paintings from Taiwan, had them framed and hung them on the walls. My parents took turns greeting the restaurant guests and showing them to their tables. My father always wore a white shirt and tie. He fastened the cuffs with cufflinks of jade Buddhas. My mother, who maintained a slim figure even in her sixties, always wore patent leather pumps and a cheongsam. In the winter they were sewn from a heavy silk brocade. In the summer they had short sleeves and were made of fine cotton, often with a flower print. Her prize jade pendant dangled from a heavy gold chain around her neck. When my mother showed signs of turning grey, she immediately started to dye her hair. She now possessed an ageless look. Her face lightly powdered and her black eyebrows skilfully drawn in the same shape as Elizabeth Taylor's.

The Woo's restaurant, The Golden Gate, had a spacious dining room. At the back was a large room divider decorated with a golden dragon and phoenix, moulded in relief. Behind this was the entrance to the kitchen. The waitresses wore mustard-coloured uniforms with short white aprons — semi-circles with ruffles around the edge. The lighting in the Woo's restaurant was always bright, whereas ours was dimmed. The atmosphere in the Woo's restaurant seemed casual and open. Ours, I suppose, was meant to be enticing. Mrs Woo, who was round-faced and thick set, never possessed my mother's dramatic flair in clothing. Throughout my childhood I only remember seeing her in A-line skirts and white short-sleeved blouses with Peter Pan collars. In the winter she wore a beige cardigan with pearl buttons.

The rivalry was never out in the open. After all, the two families got together at Christmas, Chinese New Year and barbecues during the summer. But each lay hidden in ambush, ready to politely belittle the other's success and secretly relish the other's failure. They competed in business and — for even higher stakes — with their children. My brother David and I against Jean and Bobby. Mrs Woo still had twelve-year-old Helen at home; but, she being so much younger didn't count when it came to the tally of scores. Although the Woos had the edge when it came to business, my mother clearly had the upper hand when it came to the children. My brother and I were both good-looking, excellent students, Ontario scholars, winners of academic prizes. Our winning point, though, was that we both spoke perfect unaccented English. This probably had more to do with the fact that we were both born here, than with any intrinsic linguistic ability. My mother used to brag, "If you'd never met them and just spoke to them on the phone, you'd never know that either was Chinese." On the other hand, Jean, who came to Canada at age nine, spoke English with a slight but obvious accent, forever marking her as a foreigner. She would never be able to hide behind a telephone line. And her older brother, Bobby, never even finished high school. He would have no choice but to carry on the family business. My mother and Gladys Woo often joked about me and Bobby one day getting married. Once it became apparent that I was to continue in school and would not settle for a life in the restaurant business, Gladys said to my mother, "Well, when Bobby gets married, I'll find him a big girl. She's going to be so tall, when she falls she makes a sound." My mother knew that this was a thinly cloaked barb aimed at her daughter, who was barely five feet tall. But my mother apparently said nothing, recognizing the sour grapes for what they were. She knew she had the upper hand. Her daughter was moving up, soon to be high class, a member of a profession.

But now the tables were turned and Jean was getting married. To make matters worse, Jean had snared herself a doctor. Mrs Woo could now bask in her daughter's newly elevated status and look forward to even more grandchildren.

I had first learned about Jean getting married three months ago. I was visiting my parents in their new suburban home in Urquhart. Several years earlier, my father had sold his business for a handsome price, and now he spent his time maintaining his rental properties and gardening. I was at the kitchen table helping my mother make wontons when she suddenly said to me,

"You marry someone Chinese. Only someone Chinese knows what it means to be Chinese," as she placed a dollop of pork and shrimp filling in the middle of the wonton wrapper.

Mah, this is Canada. The people here don't think like that. At least that's what I wanted to say. Instead I opted for something safe. "I'm not even thinking about marriage. When I finish my degree, I'm going to graduate school." My eyes remained downcast as I placed a small spoonful of the minced meat in the middle of my wonton wrapper. The amount of filling had to be just right. Too much and the pouch would burst, too little and people would think you were cheap. Next I dipped my finger in the rice bowl filled with water, and then started to wet the edges of the wrapper. As I put my finger in the bowl a second time my mother called out, "Don't put on so much water. The pastry will get all soggy." The edges of the wrapper were brought together to make a triangle. The two bottom corners were brought together to form a circle, and then the top corner was pushed through the opening. The final result looked a little like the crown of an Egyptian pharaoh. My mother was always disdainful of those people who brought the four corners of the wonton square together and cinched the pastry at the top of the filling. It was a display of laziness and a lack of artistry. When I finished my little creation I carefully added it to the rows of wontons on the rectangular tray in the middle of my mother's red arborite table. My mother smiled indulgently at me, for her wontons were perfect creations. The edges were perfectly matched and the apex of each triangular crown pointed straight up. Next to hers, mine were by no means misshapen, if so, only slightly, but obviously, "not perfect."

Mah continued. "Jean Woo is getting married next month to a doctor. He has a practice in Urquhart. I met her mother last week at Lucky People's grocery store when your father drove me to Toronto."

"Oh? That's nice. When's the big date?"

Mah ignored my question. "Do you know what she said to me?"

My mother switched to a higher register as she mimicked her friend's voice. Her body leaned forward, but her head turned away from me, as if she was speaking to an imaginary Gladys.

"'Sorry, ah, Choy *syeem*, but I really don't have time to talk. I'm so busy these days. Not lucky like you, no children at home, no grandchildren, all your time to yourself. Me, I'm so busy looking after Bobby and Valerie's baby. Helen's not even in high school yet. And getting ready for the wedding! You have no idea how hard my life has become now that I'm a grandmother, and now with Jean getting married. It's going to be at the Pearl Court in Toronto. Not too high class. Very simple, only about six hundred people. I hope everybody in your family will be able to come. I know it'll be hard for David, going to school in B.C. But Jean will really want to see Nancy. By the way, how's Nancy? Does she have a boyfriend yet?' Well, I wasn't going to let her get the better of me. I just said to her 'Nancy doesn't have time to think about marriage. She still has another year of university. The teachers say she's very smart. Some of them even want her to get a master's degree.' And then do you know what she said? 'Well, I guess if you can't get a boyfriend you might as well go to school. But you should tell Nancy that men don't like girls who are too well educated.'" My mother then turned to me, her expression a blend of frustration and indignation. "Oh, that Gladys just makes me so mad! Just because she has a grandson, and now Jean, that horse-face girl is going to have a big fancy wedding and a reception at an expensive restaurant."

As I listened, I tried to maintain a thoughtful expression on my face. But in fact it didn't matter. My mother was too caught up in the telling to notice that I was trying to repress a smile. In my mind I could see her face as she received this news from Gladys, who would of course be smiling a superior smile, pointedly, but humbly informing my mother of their new family conquests. A reception for six hundred people at the most expensive restaurant in Chinatown was a feather in Gladys's cap that refused to be ignored. And her growing concern about me served only to make my mother's fury more fierce. Yet a part of me felt responsible for my mother's hidden pain. I wasn't giving her grandchildren so that she, too, could complain about the difficulty of her life.

At this point in her conversation with Gladys, my mother decided to play her ace. Everyone knew that Jean was getting married to a *lo fon*, a white man. Her family had not been pleased. However, the fact that he was a doctor with a flourishing practice meant that he was fairly quickly accepted. "So you know what I said to her? 'Nancy isn't going to marry a *gwei loh*, a ghost man. When it's time for her to choose she will pick a Chinese. She wouldn't marry a *gwei loh*. She has too much respect for me.'"

"Ma-ah!" I exclaimed in complete exasperation, as I tossed the metal spoon into the near empty bowl of filling, making a loud ringing clang. But my mother carried on as if she hadn't heard a thing.

"In a way I feel sorry for Gladys. She's not going to be able to talk to her big shot son-in-law, you know. She can't speak English and he can't speak Chinese. And when they have children, the children won't speak Chinese, you know. They won't know anything about being Chinese. They're going to be able to say anything they want in front of her. They won't even want Gladys around." She picked up a wooden spatula and started to scrape together the filling stuck to the side of the bowl. There was just enough minced meat left for one last wonton.

"Mah, how can you say that? You don't know."

"Nancy, you're the one who doesn't know. Once Jean's married, Gladys will hardly ever see her." My mother stood up and carried the tray of finished wontons to the counter next to the stove.

"But Mah, just because Jean's getting married to a *lo fon*, doesn't mean she's going to forget about her own family." I started to carry the dishes over to the stove. My mother carefully dropped the finished wontons into a pot of boiling water as she continued talking.

"Oh, it's not that Jean doesn't care about her mother. But once she's married to a *gwei loh* she'll be spending all her time with *lo fons*. She'll forget about being Chinese. I know. Jean will want to spend all her time with her *lo fon* family. She'll forget all about being Chinese. I know." Afterwards my mother drained the cooked wontons and placed them in a swirling broth made from pork and chicken bones. I knew from a certain stiffness in her shoulders that the discussion was over.

The few times that I had brought a white boy home, my mother always hovered about, leaving and then returning with plates of sliced oranges, bunches of grapes and sweet biscuits. With a stiff smile on her face, she interrupted with her litany of English phrases: "More pop?" "Eat more." "You want some more?"

When my *lo fon* boyfriends left, or when I returned home from a date, my mother never failed to remind me, "Nothing wrong with being friends with a *lo fon*, but you should never marry one. You'd be asking for trouble. Think about your children. They wouldn't really belong to us Chinese or to the *lo fons*."

I always wanted to meet my mother head on. "Well, why not? There's nothing wrong with *lo fons*. They're people just like us. Anyway, there aren't any Chinese guys in Urquhart. And I'm sure as hell not going to let you get one from the matchmaker. This is Canada, not China". But my tongue always seemed to thicken, as the words caught in the dryness of my throat. My response became standard: "There's nothing to worry about. We're just friends. I'm not serious about anyone. I want to finish my education before I even think about getting married."

Of course, what my mother was trying to get from me was reassurance that I would not marry outside our race. Our lives in Canada, as far as she was concerned, were already overrun by *gwei*, ghosts — *gwei* men, *gwei* women, *gwei* children. We served food to *gwei* customers, bought from *gwei* shopkeepers, were treated by *gwei* doctors and taught by *gwei* teachers.

When I was a child it was confusing because she talked about ghosts back in China. Were they like the ones here? the ones that I saw everyday and spoke to? the ones who were my teacher and my best friend?

My mother finished counting the attendants and was now furtively looking around to see who was at the wedding. She nudged me in the side and motioned with her head. "Look, there's Edward Lim." I looked blankly at her and shrugged my shoulders. "Don't you know? Edward Lim, the developer from Hong Kong!" she whispered in exasperated tones. I nodded my head and turned to watch Jean finish her slow walk down the aisle on her father's arm. While Jean was exchanging her marriage vows, I started thinking about my mother's story of the farmer and his ghost bride. I had listened to this tale all my life. The people in my mother's stories were never what they seemed. The stories were like labyrinths. In the back of my mind there always floated unanswered questions. What does this mean? Where does it lead to? But suddenly I was viewing the farmer and his bride through a new lens, one that was in focus, allowing me to see more clearly. I couldn't help smiling. Was I finally beginning to understand what this story meant to my mother?

When we arrived at the Pearl Court for Jean's reception, my mother sat stiffly while she and my father made polite conversation with the other guests at our table. Sitting across the table from my mother were Mrs Yee, the matchmaker, and her husband. As a younger woman, Mrs Yee had been responsible for arranging many marriages in Chinatown, locally and by mail-order. To supplement her matchmaking income, she also sewed beads and sequins on gowns and jackets for fancy dress shops. Over the years, what had started as a way to make a little extra money had been transformed into a lucrative business. She now had a small shop on Dundas Street that advertised her bead and sequin work. These days, the real money was made from selling rough, lumpy beads made of clay, wood and shells to unkempt-looking young people with long hair, scruffy jeans and shapeless flowered skirts. But Mrs Yee still performed the occasional matching of hearts.

My mother recognized Mrs Yee immediately and smiled weakly at her. Mrs Yee smiled broadly as she leaned towards her. "And this is your daughter? Very pretty."

"Yes, oh, so so," My mother acknowledged, falsely modest.

"And when is she getting married?"

"No time for boyfriend. Too busy going to school." My mother shook her head and fidgeted with her gold bangles as she spoke.

Mrs Yee then looked at me. "You want a boyfriend? I know one I can introduce you to. Good family. Lots of money."

"That's very kind of you, but...."

Before I was able to finish my mother interrupted. "I say good idea. But you know young people today. Don't listen to us anymore. They want to arrange their own marriages." Mrs Yee smiled and shrugged her shoulders as she and my mother exchanged a glance of mutual understanding and resignation. Then they both turned to the elderly guests at our table and started to heap onto their plates the choicest morsels from each dish, each trying to outdo the other in their concern for the well-being of others.

Everyone *oohed* and *ahhed* at each new course. There were delicately flavoured shark's fin soup, lobster with ginger, deep fried oysters, gently stirred fried scallops served in a crispy taro basket, smooth juicy white chicken with scallions, and more. From these dishes it was clear that Jean's reception was expensive, but the garnishes elevated it into something exceptional. The plates weren't simply accentuated with leaves of lettuce or sprigs of parsley, but arrived accompanied by dragons, swans, fans, flowers, each item exquisitely carved and intricately fashioned from carrots, white and red radishes, cucumbers and green onions. Chopsticks moved gingerly around each ornament, taking care not to get too close, making sure that it remained still and pristine in its sacred position.

There was no doubt that Jean's wedding was a triumph for the Woos. When the wedding party came to our table to exchange greetings, Mrs Woo said to my mother, "Soon Nancy will be next."

But my mother would not have any of that. She wasn't going to give Gladys the satisfaction of being generous. "Oh, I don't think so. Nancy has more important things to think about. She's far too busy with school." Then they both laughed.

If my mother had known how prophetic her words would be, she might not have given them voice. She had to wait for another fifteen years and suffer through a Ph.D., before I was married. During that long wait, she never missed an opportunity to remind me that Gladys Woo now had two grandchildren, then three, then four, then five. Although my brother had been married for more than eight years to a lovely Chinese woman, there were no children.

One day, when Jean had been married for several years, my mother was visiting with Gladys when Jean dropped by with her *gwei loh* husband and her two half-*ghost* children. That evening, my mother made a point of phoning me. "I saw Jean at her mother's today."

"Oh? How's she doing?"

"She was with her husband and her two little kids."

"Did you have a nice visit."

"Her husband is very nice. Spends a lot of time with the children. Doesn't talk much, though."

"Well, of course. He can't speak Chinese and Gladys doesn't speak English."

"Gladys only sees them once every few weeks, you know."

"But Mah, they live an hour and a half away. They're very busy." There was a slight pause. In my mind I could see her weighing her thoughts before speaking.

"If Jean had married a Chinese, they'd probably visit her mother more."

"Mah!"

"They have beautiful children, though."

"I'm sure they do."

"You know the one thing I do have to say about half-*ghost* children is that they are beautiful. They get the best of both. But Jean's children have been especially lucky. Neither of them got her horse-shaped face."

When I finally got married, I was thirty-eight years old. The fact that I, too, was marrying a *gwei loh*, a ghost man, had become irrelevant. For my mother, the shame and humiliation of having an unmarried daughter quickly approaching forty had become almost unbearable. She was also convinced that no Chinese male in his right mind would want to marry an over-educated woman nearing the end of her child-bearing years.

On the day of my wedding my mother helped me with my wedding gown. It was a sheath of white fluid silk with long narrow sleeves, outstanding in its simplicity except for the forty-eight pearl buttons down the back. There were forty-eight loops, delicately woven from strands of silk, each of which had to be slipped over a button. My mother carefully pulled each loop over each opalescent head. I could feel the opening of the dress gradually close. And as my mother's fingers worked deftly, she told me once again the story of the young farmer and his ghost wife. She finished the story just as the last loop was slipped over the head of the last button. As I listened to her words, my jaw and fists became clenched, as if stiffening would shut my pores and prevent the rage building up in my body from escaping. I wanted to scream, *Why are you telling me that story? Why today of all days? Can't you for once put aside your fears and accept? Can't you just let go? I'm not going to forget about you.* When my mother finished with my dress, she straightened herself up and dropped her hands to her sides. I turned abruptly and glared at her face. Her eyes were wet with a film of tears. I saw in them not just the fear and hunger of the young farmer, but suddenly, a reflection of fear and hunger that was my own. The words that were ready to burst like a volley of bullets from my lips vanished. All my anger dissolved. I put my arms around her, and for a moment we held each other and said nothing.

8

CHINA DOG

WEI JOON CHONG SAT DOWN AT THE KITCHEN TABLE FOR lunch and saw before him in a chipped bowl, a lifeless lump of shiny rice, sticking together like a mass of mushy, white, glutinous dough. His wife had purposely committed this act of treachery to stir up his loathing. He knew it. That Lai Yung dared to insult him so soon after his eightieth birthday was more than he could stand. Lai Yung knew that when properly cooked, each rice kernel should be soft, yet stand out separately from all the others. His heart pounding, his head throbbing, Wei Joon looked up and saw Lai Yung's stare, pretending innocence, secretly gloating.

"You bitch! Look at this rice. Overcooked, all stuck together. Fit for a pig!"

"Oh, don't be ridiculous," said his wife. She picked up her bowl and started to shovel the rice in her mouth with her chopsticks. "Everything's fine. You're imagining things, old man."

Wei Joon stood up shaking. He was dripping with perspiration, his undershirt clinging to his body. The Chinese radio station was on. He could hear the news announcer in the background. Something about dragon boats, races, the Toronto Islands. Each word hung in the air, alone, without meaning. The drone of the voice was irritating. He wanted it off, but where was the radio? His mind was separating from his body. Where were his hands? His elbows? He looked down and saw a soup bowl lying on its side, the broth spilling out over the faded, mottled beige arborite, and then dripping over the chipped chrome edge of the table. Was that his soup? Had he done that?

"You clumsy old man! Look what you've done. As if I don't have enough to do!" Lai Yung grabbed the dishcloth from the sink.

Wei Joon pushed the wooden chair from behind him and rushed down the wooden stairs into the basement. Lai Yung shouted after him. He didn't understand any of her words. Everything was a jumble of angry sounds, sharp jabs piercing his body.

Lai Yung picked up her bowl again and started to carefully eat her rice. The silence grew, filling the room like smoke from a burning pot. Suddenly she dropped her bowl and chopsticks onto the table and rushed down the basement stairs. She moved with such speed that she might have smashed into the wall had her momentum not been interrupted by a pair of legs dangling in the air.

"Eiiiiyah! Oh my God, my God..." Lai Yung looked up and saw Wei Joon hanging like a puppet with a rope around his neck. The head was slack and slumped at a strange angle on his chest. Her hand shot up to her mouth when she saw the protruding eyes and the wide gaping mouth. But her heart lurched, cramped, when she realized the lips had frozen with just a hint of a smile, triumphantly mocking her.

Then she saw the chair, knocked over, lying on its side. Lai Yung's heart pounded heavily and her breath grew short as she righted the chair. She was trembling uncontrollably. She climbed up and wrapped her arms around his scrawny thighs, attempting to lift the body, slacken the rope from which he hanged. He was still warm.

Dan-Mu sat between his wife, Lee Ming, and his stepmother, Lai Yung.

They were sitting on the first pew, inside the chapel at the Wen Ing Funeral Home on College Street in Toronto. His stepmother was weeping. Lee Ming sat with her hands gripped in a tight, tense knot. Her head was bowed, but her eyes were darting furtively about. Wei Joon was laid out in the casket at the head of the chapel. Even in death he looked uncomfortable. The suit was slightly too large. He looked out of place in the luxury of a polished mahogany coffin, his body surrounded and cushioned by soft folds of shiny satin. In front of the open casket was an altar with an offering to the ancestors. As people came into the chapel, they stood before the altar, lit sticks of incense and placed them in the brass urn next to a plate of cooked white chicken. They walked to the casket and bowed three times before Wei Joon. Then the mourners turned and exchanged awkward expressions of sympathy with the grieving family members before quickly returning to their pews.

Everywhere Lee Ming looked, she saw vases and wreaths of flowers — gladioli, carnations, chrysanthemums and roses, mostly white, some in varying shades of yellow. It was an unexpected display. The old man was not popular in the community. He was known for his ill-temper. She heard the minister's words in the background. Her mind drifted in and out, catching phrases of his service. Her father-in-law had endured an immigrant's life, a life of hard work and sacrifice. To him, his children owed the life they now enjoyed. But no one was listening. They were all immersed in their own thoughts, the same thoughts. Why did he do this? An act of anger? Revenge? Spite? Was this his final statement?

Lee Ming looked around at the funeral gathering. The pew behind her and the one beside were filled with immediate family members. They were a collection of half-and step-sib-lings, having arrived in Canada at different times. Usually the Chongs bore no resemblance to each other. But today grief had painted them with the same dark brush. Even the family bohemian had abandoned her leather sandals and full floral Indian skirts for nylon stockings, black pumps and a plain black dress. Their heads were bowed, eyes cast down, shoul-ders hunched. Eye contact was fleeting. Everyone was wrapped in sombre cloth. Shame connected them more powerfully than blood.

There had been rumours about Lee Ming's father-in-law and his family. She sat twisting her hands, trying to remember. It was something that had happened a long time ago, some-thing about someone back in China hanging himself. Was this family that she had married into really cursed by suicide? In the background she heard the monotone of the minister's words, but in her mind the whispers from the congregation thundered. The two women in the pew behind were whisper-ing. Lee Ming turned and glared at them. One of the women looked up and caught Ming's stare. The woman averted her eyes and stopped talking.

When Ming was twelve years old and living in China, an old woman dressed in rags wandered into her village. Ming was laughing and gossiping with a friend outside the compound wall that enclosed their homes. Her friend suddenly tapped Ming on the shoulder. Ming turned and saw the old woman walking directly towards her, like a menacing stormcloud of grey rags flapping in the air. She stopped in front of Ming and stared at her. Ming stood frozen, unable to move, barely able to breathe. The old woman spoke without blinking in an icy monotone, her breath like sour meat, her words like shards of glass. "For a long time you will think you are happy, but beware, for the scorpion of misfortune rides on your back." The old woman turned and started to walk away. Ming ran after her, "What do you mean? Who are you?" But the old woman kept walking, facing straight ahead. Ming collapsed and started to sob. Her friend ran inside the compound and rushed out with Ming's mother. They ran up and down the dirt road. But the old woman was nowhere to be seen.

Her mother quickly swept Ming back inside the house. Ming sat in the kitchen, watching her mother rush erratically about, first pouring a cup of tepid tea for her daughter, then looking through her shelves for the jar of rock sugar, muttering all the while, "No fear, no fear. Just a silly old woman." But Ming saw her slop the tea as she poured and heard the shortness in her breath. As Ming sipped the tea with the rock sugar melting in her mouth, she knew the sweetness of the candy was but a flimsy talisman against the old woman's words. Someone from another world had reached into their lives with a frightening pronouncement, casting a shadow over Ming's life. From that moment on, Ming faced the world with her head turned to the side, longing for the security of the past, dreading the uncertainty of the future.

The minister asked everyone to stand and pray. Ming rose and looked at Dan-Mu standing beside her, his jaw tightly clenched, his face impassive. Gradually, she was remembering more details of the rumour. It was about Wei Joon's grandfather. He hung himself too. That was it. There was something about a landlord back in China placing a curse on the family. But why? Was this family really cursed by suicide? Ming turned and glanced again at Dan-Mu. The words of the ghost woman from her childhood resonated inside her head. "Beware, the scorpion of misfortune rides on your back." Her eyes widened with sudden horror. Dan was next. She knew it. A revelation. No one needed to tell her in words or write it down on paper. Again she looked at her husband, this piece of dormant organic knowledge sprouting, rooting, branching into every corner and crevice of her being. It was as real and irrefutable as the floor beneath her feet.

Ming and her two children stood outside the door of their house, watching Dan fiddle with the key. Once inside, they all bent down and took off their shoes before putting on their Chinese slippers. For six years they had lived on the first floor of this house, and rented the second and third floors to other families. Over the last few days there had been little contact. Ming knew that her tenants were deliberately avoiding them. Their whispering stopped when they caught sight of her. Bad news in Chinatown spread like fire on a windy day. She understood their discomfort. What do you say when someone has hanged himself? Somehow the sympathies that were usually expressed seemed ill-fitting. Did he go peacefully?

Ming stood by her sink rinsing out the rice. Tonight's dinner would be simple. Leftover chicken and oxtail soup from yesterday. She would stir-fry some greens. They had had a good meal at the reception after the funeral. Fortunately no one would be very hungry.

There was little conversation as they sat down together at the kitchen table. Ming looked at her son who was twelve; her daughter, fifteen. They were both strong, healthy, well-adjusted children and excellent students. That description fit all their cousins as well. Then why did that old man go and hang himself? Didn't he recognize good fortune? Was he fighting with his wife again? But they were fighting even before Ming married into the family. Their anger towards each other was the engine that propelled their marriage. Was it spite? Did he just want to have the last word? One final gesture that would leave his wife defeated?

"Ming, is there any more soup?"

"Oh. Oh, yes, Dan. I'll get some. Do you want some more rice?" Ming took her husband's rice bowl without waiting for an answer. As she handed him the refilled bowl, she saw a crease around his neck that she had never noticed before. For a moment she stood mesmerized, watching his adam's apple move above and below the line as he chewed and swallowed his food. She had to control an impulse to put her fingers around his neck, to stretch the skin and make the crease disappear.

After the supper dishes and the Chinese evening news, Ming started to prepare for bed. Dan was already in the bathtub. Ming stood in front of the bathroom mirror, concentrating on the circular motion of her toothbrush.

"Ming, don't take it so hard. You've been so quiet all evening." Dan got out of the bathtub and started to dry himself. Ming rinsed her mouth and spat the water into the sink. "You've hardly said a thing. This place is starting to feel like a morgue."

Until that moment, Ming hadn't realized how self-absorbed she was being. She turned abruptly and faced her husband. "Dan, you don't suppose what those old ladies are saying might be true?" Ming started to change into her pyjamas. She carefully folded her clothes and placed them on a chair in the corner of their bedroom.

"What are they saying?"

"That your family's cursed. That suicide runs in your family."

"And what does that mean?" Dan finished putting on his pyjamas and got into bed.

"Dan isn't there something about a landlord cursing your great-grandfather who ended up hanging himself?"

"Oh, that. My mother told me the local landlord used to cheat the tenant farmers by rigging the scales. My great-grandfather was routinely paid next to nothing for his harvests of oats. Apparently, he got so angry, he kidnapped the landlord's prize Pekinese. Then he chopped it into chunks, put everything into a pot and put it on the landlord's doorstep. Only he didn't do it right away. He waited for several days until the meat started to rot and stink. Nobody was able to prove that it was my great-grandfather. He was just the prime suspect. Probably because he was the loudest about his anger."

"So then the landlord cursed the family?"

"That's never been proven. But when the old man hung himself, the village said it was the landlord's curse."

"Well, people are whispering that your family is cursed."

"Is that what you're worried about? Don't be ridiculous. This is Canada."

"But Dan.... What if?"

"Ming, stop worrying. Life in China was hard. And my father was always unhappy here. Things are different now. I've no intention of wearing a rope around my neck. Now or in the future." Ming got into bed next to her husband. Dan could tell that the notion of suicide running in the family had embedded itself in her mind. He put an arm around her. She was biting the right corner of her lower lip. When she did that, there was no hope of distracting her.

"C'mon Ming. Give your mind a rest."

Ming said nothing. A few moments later, when Dan turned toward her and climbed on top of her body, her fingers gently touched the creases around his neck. The folds wove together like a rope. Was it her imagination?

Two days later, Ming left for work. She waited for the streetcar at the corner of Queen and Greenwood. It wasn't particularly crowded that morning. Ming found a seat at the back. Her head felt congested. Not with mucus, but with that single thought: that Dan was next. She had felt the rope of creases. Earlier that morning she'd had to stop herself from suggesting to Dan that he wear a turtleneck. It was a hot day in June. She had to be careful. It was hard to know when a ridiculous idea like that might come tumbling out of her mouth. Other thoughts entered Ming's mind, but soon they were pushed aside and her obsession with the family curse edged its way back. Not abruptly like thunder, but insidious-ly like fog. Suddenly her mind was filled and she couldn't see anything else. Ming couldn't even remember what she made for the children's lunches. Did she make ham sandwiches, or did she use the left over barbecued pork?

Ming got off the streetcar at Queen and Spadina. She walked south to Wellington. Her factory was just half a block from the corner. It had just received a new contract for mak-ing women's coats. Her job was to do the hems. She was thankful for that. Even though it meant handling the whole coat, which was heavy, at least it wasn't finicky work, like binding buttonholes. The trademark of a high-class coat was its bound buttonholes. And these were high-class. On a bound buttonhole, the seams were neatly tucked inside and all the stitching was hidden. On cheaper coats they were stitched on the machine and then somebody slit the opening.

Ming had already decided that she would talk to Wong Mo, old Mrs Wong, at morning break. Mrs Wong was in her sixties. When she was widowed five years back, she had mourned appropriately, but it was obvious that she was freed by the death of her elderly, demanding husband. She lived on the first floor of her Huron Street home and rented out the five rooms on the second and third floors.

When Mrs Wong arrived in Canada in 1954 with her twelve-year-old son, she had not seen her husband for seven years. Mrs Wong had lived in Chinatown for over thirty years. She was unable to read or write. Yet she knew the location and was able to describe the front of every shop in Chinatown. She knew the colour of the doors, the frames, and the decorations on the signs. Her body seemed to pos-sess some kind of inner radar that instinctively directed her to the lowest prices in Chinatown. She had the goods on every young woman of marriageable age and had in mind an appropriate young man for each. Ming knew that with Mrs Wong there was nothing to hide. She could assume that Mrs Wong knew the circumstances of her father-in-law's death and that by now would have heard the rumours of the curse. Ming decided not to confide her concern that Dan was next. She didn't want that speculation flying around Chinatown. She would start by asking for general advice on how to stop the curse.

Ming paused outside her building and sighed. It had been ten days since the suicide. She hadn't found out about the old man's hanging until she arrived home that night. But her mother-in-law had called Dan as soon as she cut the old man down. Dan had to deal with his stepmother's hysteria. He called 911 and went in the ambulance with his dead father. There, he explained in his broken English to the officious doctors that his father, at age eighty, had hung himself.

Although Ming dreaded going back to work, a small part of her welcomed it. It meant returning to routines. Perhaps an opportunity to do something about this curse that was haunting her family. Ming opened the heavy wooden door of her building and walked down the half-flight of stairs to the sewing room where she worked. Her machine was in the third row. She felt lucky about being close to the window. In the summer, she could at least open one of the lower panes and feel the breeze from outside.

Most of the women were seated at their sewing machines. When they caught Ming's eye, they cautiously nodded. She sat down at her machine, checked the thread and started her work.

At break time, Ming walked up the aisle to Mrs Wong's station. She took her thermos with her and offered her a cup of oolong tea. Mrs Wong didn't work at a sewing machine. Pieces of finished clothing were piled at her table. Her job was to snip off the dangling pieces of excess thread. Mrs Wong moved over on her bench and motioned for Ming to sit down. Ming looked up and saw her friends Elsie Low and Mary Chow who had been at the funeral. They gave her a quick hug and leaned against the sewing table.

"Ah, Ming. I am so sorry." Mrs Wong patted her on the arm.

Ming took a deep breath. "Wong *Mo*, you know what people are saying about my husband's family?"

"I know, Ming."

"Wong *Mo*, I'm afraid the curse is real. I want to stop it."

"Oh Ming, do you really think that? I mean this is Canada," said Elsie.

"Well, Elsie, I don't want to take any chances." Ming didn't dare mention her premonition about Dan.

"There's no harm in taking precautions," Mrs Wong nodded as she spoke and took another sip of tea.

Mary leaned a little closer. "I think you've got a point."

Mrs Wong thought for a few seconds. "Go and visit a *sung pu*, a fortune teller. Maybe she could help you."

Two weeks later, on a Saturday morning, Ming left home early. She told her family that she was going to Chinatown to pick up groceries. What they didn't know was that she also had an appointment with Mrs Wong to visit a *sung pu*.

Ming had never been to Mrs Wong's house before. It

was early, so she found a parking spot on Beverly Street below Dundas without difficulty. As she walked past Grange Park, several homeless people were still asleep on the benches. Even though it was late June, they were wrapped in heavy winter coats. Probably to ward off the early morning chill. From a distance, it was hard to tell whether they were men or women. Their multiple layers of clothing had all taken on varying shades of brown and grey. Ming turned left on Dundas and then up Huron Street.

Mrs Wong lived in a Victorian semi-detached house. The wooden porch had settled and the floor slanted slightly. Ming rang the doorbell. As she waited, she noticed that the windows were covered with a threadbare red paisley curtain. Over the bottom half of the sash windows were taped some Chinese newspapers, yellow with age. She saw Mrs Wong peek through a peep hole that had been ripped into a corner of the newspaper. A few moments later Mrs Wong slowly opened her door. "Ah Ming. Come in and sit down for a moment." Ming stepped inside and handed Mrs Wong a bag filled with oranges.

The *sung pu* lived on Glasgow Street. Ming had no idea that the street existed. It was a city secret, tucked in the south-east corner of Spadina and College. They walked down an alley off Huron, past a three-storey orange brick apartment building. Two-storey row houses and semis stood on either side of Glasgow Street. The houses had no front lawns. The small wooden porches were flush with the treeless sidewalks. In all, there might have been a dozen homes. The *sung pu* lived in a semi of freshly-painted red bricks with a bright green porch.

The *sung pu* opened the door. She appeared to be in her mid-sixties, around the same age as Mrs Wong. In contrast to Mrs Wong who was short, round and plain, she was heavily powdered, with red lips, rouged pouchy cheeks, and thinly pencilled brows. Her hair was permed and artificially black. She wore several gold chains around her neck. One had dangling from it a large jade pendant. The gold had the pink-tinted colour of the kind bought in Hong Kong. It looked rich and pure, not like the gold bought here from the *lo fon* stores, gold that had been mixed with other metals and made to look cheap and glistening.

The *sung pu* led Ming and Mrs Wong into a tiny square landing, then up a flight of three shallow steps and down a short hallway into the kitchen. Ming handed her a bag containing several oranges and some seedless green grapes. She asked Ming and Mrs Wong to sit down at the kitchen table next to the window. The window looked out at the wall of the next house. The wall was so close that if Ming had been able to reach through the glass, she could have touched it. The *sung pu* sat down across from them and poured three cups of tea from a thermos bottle.

She looked first at Mrs Wong, then at Ming. "Chong *Tai*, Wong *Mo* has told me a little about your situation. I'm sorry about your father-in-law." Ming caught a faint whiff of the *sung pu's* breath. There was a slight, but distinctly sour smell, a smell of meat going bad.

Ming set her tea cup down and interlocked her fingers in her lap. She leaned slightly forward. She looked first at Mrs Wong, then at the *sung pu*. "Lam *Tai*, do you know how my father-in-law died?" The *sung pu* nodded. "I'm very worried that this might be a family curse." Ming hesitated, then went on. "My husband's great-grandfather also hung himself."

"Oh." The *sung pu* was obviously interested.

"If there is a family curse, I want to find a way to stop it. Can you help me?" Again, Ming made no mention of her concerns about Dan. But there was something about the way the *sung pu* stared at her that made Ming wonder if she hadn't already guessed the deeper reason for her anxiety.

"Is there any way you can get in touch with the family spirits?" asked Mrs Wong.

"I can try," said the *sung pu*. "Come back in two weeks. We should give your father-in-law a little more time to settle in with the ancestors."

"Shall I come too?" asked Mrs Wong.

"It makes no difference to me. It's up to Chong *Tai*."

It was obvious that Mrs Wong did not want to be left out. Ming nodded agreement and smiled . "Of course."

As Ming left with Mrs Wong she gave the *sung pu* a red lucky money envelope. Inside were twenty dollars.

Two weeks later, Ming and Mrs Wong were sitting in the *sung pu's* kitchen. Outside it was a brilliant sunny morning. But inside the tiny kitchen on Glasgow Street, it was dark. Ming looked through the window at the wall of the next house. The shadow that she had seen before seemed even darker, the space between the houses like a cave in half-light. She was surprised that they were there on a Saturday morning. She had expected to return in the evening. Somehow she associated conjuring up spirits with the night. She wondered if these notions were from watching too much television. After Ming gave the *sung pu* an offering of oranges and coconut candies, and after a sip of jasmine tea, she took them into the living room.

The living room was a small square room with a window overlooking Glasgow Street. Along one wall was a three-seater sofa covered in a red crushed velvet. Ming saw a matching armchair and a plastic wood-veneer coffee table. Standing in a corner was a large television set. Several Chinese newspapers and glossy magazines with close-ups of glamorous young women were scattered on the coffee table. The walls were bare, except for a clock in the shape of a jewelled phoenix. The *sung pu* drew the green and gold brocade curtains over the windows and closed the door. Ming and Mrs Wong sat down together on the red sofa. The *sung pu* pulled the coffee table away from the window and positioned it near the back of the room. On it she placed an offering of oranges and a white cooked chicken. She lit incense and thin wax candles on sticks and burned some special paper money. She sat down on the single chair and closed her eyes. Her breathing gradually became deeper and slower. Ming felt a slight change in the air and she saw the flames on the candles flicker. She and Mrs Wong watched in silence, unable to move.

Suddenly the *sung pu's* body began to twitch, then stiffen, and she sat upright in the chair. Her lips parted. Ming was shocked at the voice that came out. It was the voice of her father-in-law, sounding strained and stretched, as if someone had pulled his vocal chords until each tone was thinned in the middle. He told them that there was a curse on the family. That to end it, they would have to find a way of confusing the spirits. "But how?" asked Ming, leaning forward, her back tense. The *sung pu* went into a slump. When she opened her eyes, her face was drenched in perspiration. Breathing heavily, she dabbed her face with her handkerchief, smudging the white cloth with rouge and powder.

"But how?" Ming repeated, "how can we fool the spirits?"

The *sung pu* looked directly at Ming. "Go to a store and buy a small china dog, about the size of your hand. Come back at the same time next week."

For days Ming walked around with the porcelain china dog wrapped in tissue paper and hidden in her purse. What if she was found out? Then she would have to either lie or explain. She was only trying to protect her family. So why did she feel that her activities were questionable, like she was hiding a crime? A few days earlier, she had walked into the China Emporium and gone directly to the shelves of china figurines. Standing there, she gasped, her hand covering her open mouth. A row of porcelain, glazed-blue Pekinese dogs stared back at her. She even lied when she bought the wretched thing. She told the sales clerk that it was for her daughter — as if the clerk cared.

Ming and Mrs Wong were standing inside the *sung pu's* living room. The curtains were drawn and the door was closed. There was an offering to the ancestors on the coffee table. On the floor was a galvanized metal pail, half-filled with water. Ming's hand shook as she gave the *sung pu* the china dog. The three women crouched around the basin. The *sung pu* took a thin rope from her pocket and tied it around the neck of the china dog. She dangled the object over the pail of water. Then she grasped the dog in her hand and smashed it against the side of the pail. Ming winced.

"Now your family spirits will be fooled. They will think someone has taken his own life and won't look any more for somebody to fulfil the curse."

"Are we finished?" asked Ming. She looked at the shards of china floating in the water. The neck was still attached to the head and the rope was around it.

"We need to bury this. We can do it in my backyard," answered the *sung pu*. "Then you can go."

Before Ming and Mrs Wong left, the *sung pu* gave them each a coconut candy. It was as if they had been at a funeral. The sugar would sweeten their future after a bitter experience. Ming gave the *sung pu* a white envelope. Inside were two lucky, red-coloured, fifty dollar bills.

After the ceremony, Ming took Mrs Wong for *dim sum*. They left each other at the streetcar stop.

Ming sat down beside an open window on the Queen streetcar. The breeze through the window felt soothing on her face. She was exhausted, coated in a thin film of oily perspiration. She had expected to feel an enormous rush of relief. She remembered Mrs Wong's words of reassurance. "Now Ming, you can relax. Go on with life." But she still had nagging doubts. She had wanted a concrete statement, a sign that said, "The curse is finished. It's been defeated."

Ming didn't know when she became aware of the sound of sirens. As the streetcar approached her stop, the sirens grew louder. Through her window, she saw a group of people gathered around a police car and an ambulance. Traffic was at a standstill. Ming stepped out of the car through the middle doors, feeling a rush of heat from the asphalt road. She walked towards the crowd.

Was that Dan talking to the police? His mouth was trembling and his eyes were filled with fear. Ming quickened her steps and started to run. She pushed her way through the crowd, her voice rising in a panic shrill, "Dan! Dan!" A pair of strong arms abruptly stopped her.

Then Dan called out. "My wife, my wife!" And the policeman released her. Dan put his arms around her and held tightly as Ming looked at the body lying on the road. The head was at a strange angle to the body. There was blood all over. But Ming stared at a line of blood that travelled down the ear lobe and around the neck. The body belonged to her son. Ming held her hands over her mouth in horror. She loosened Dan's grip and together they knelt down beside their son. Ming started to sob, her body shaking uncontrollably. Then she turned to Dan. "What happened?"

"A dog dashed out in front of a car. Peter ran out to push the dog out of the way. I don't know why he did that. He didn't even know the dog."

Ming gently stroked Peter's blood-soaked hair. Dan put his arms around her again and she pressed her face into his shoulder. Again she turned and looked at her son. His body was frozen into an ugly, contorted position. The muscles in her abdomen twisted and tightened, forming a hard, heavy knot in the pit of her stomach. She knew that this weight would be with her for the rest of her life, that her life would never again be the same. She now knew with certainty that she had deflected the curse from her husband, but the scorpion's tail had stung.

ACKNOWLEDGEMENTS

I AM INDEBTED to many people for helping me with this book,

In particular I wish to thank Makeda Silvera for giving me a chance and deciding to publish my stories. Nadia Halim for guiding me through the rewrites with care, patience and insight. Margie Adam for the haunting, exquisite cover. Stephanie Martin for the beautiful design of the book. Helen Porter who saw my stories in their embryonic form and encouraged me to continue. Wayson Choy for his wisdom, generosity and for somehow always asking the right questions. And last but not least, Michael, Alison and Katherine.

ABOUT THE AUTHOR

J UDY FONG BATES is a writer, teacher and storyteller. Her stories have been broadcast on CBC radio and published in *Fireweed: A Feminist Quarterly*, *This Magazine* and *The Canadian Forum*.

Born in China, she came to Canada as a young child, grew up in several small Ontario towns, and now lives in Toronto with her family.

Printed in the United States
by Baker & Taylor Publisher Services